In My Mind's 'I'

An adventure...

By Paul Keller

First Published in Great Britain in 2007
by Goliath Publishing
First e-book edition was first published in 2011
by Goliath Publishing

Reissued in 2014

USA Edition printed by CreateSpace 2014

ISBN 978 0 9558418 0 4

www.goliathpublishing.co.uk
or
www.goliathpublishing.com

*Dedicated to my family,
friends and all on the path
of life's great adventure ...*

Map
Dronagon's Domain

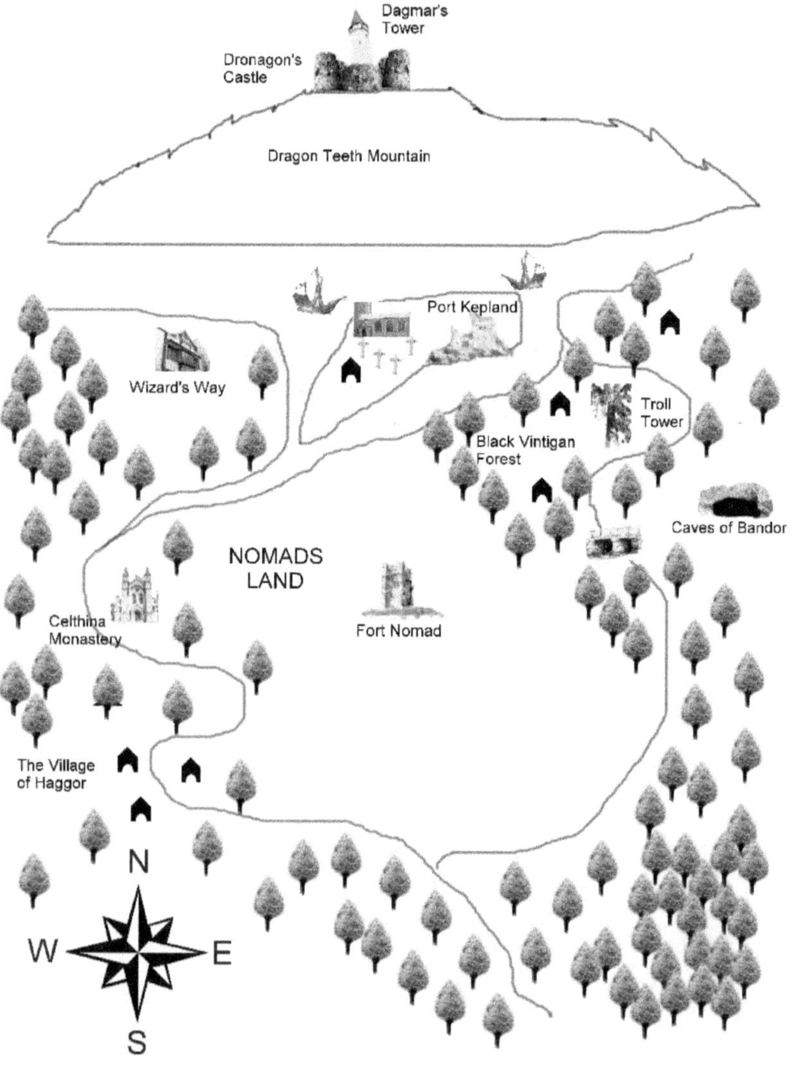

Contents

Chapter 1
In the Beginning

"Paz 'ave ye feed ta pigs yet?" shouted Beth, Pazamor's mother, a large, rounded but pretty woman, hardened by the harshness of life. Pazamor, an only child, lived alone with his mother, as his father had been killed in the Devian War when he was just five summers old.

"Just a moment!" yelled Pazamor, as he quickly blew out a small candle on his wooden bedside table and hid the shabby, old book that he had been trying to read under the dirty pillow of straw, that made part of his bed.

"Com on Paz love, we aven't got all day!" she screamed up the stairs. "Pig's got to eat ye know."

Pazamor opened the battered trap door of the attic, rushed down the creaky, wooden steps from the tiny attic space in which he slept. He blinked in the bright morning light that greeted him, slipping near the bottom of the stairs and landing on his backside with a thud! He rubbed himself quickly to avoid the oncoming pain, proceeded to the small kitchen and grabbed a filthy, wooden bucket containing the leftovers of food from the day before, which stood on the floor by the door.

His mother worked hard selling bread to the locals in the village and any burnt bits the pigs got to enjoy. These were usually the pieces that Pazamor had unsuccessfully tried to bake. He added some water to the now hardened bread and swirled it all around with a large wooden spoon, before throwing it into the pigs' trough. They crowded around in a mad frenzy, making loud oinking noises and pushing each other out of the way to get there first, almost knocking Pazamor over in their mad excitement.

"Can ye get me some eggs and don't forget to repair ta fence too."

"Ok mother!"

Pazamor went into the small hen pen, opened the door to a tiny wooden hut and lifted a few hens from their nests. After a bit of protest he managed to find two small brown and white spotted eggs. They were warm to the touch and just what they needed for breakfast! He ran into the kitchen and put the eggs in a very small metal pot with a wooden handle, filled it with water from a large bucket and left it by the open fire in the middle of the room for his mother to cook.

Pazamor returned to the yard to work on repairing the broken fence. He was very good at repairing things and everyone who knew him well would ask such favours of him.

While he set to work on mending the pigs' fence he began to ponder. He thought back to the book he had been reading earlier… *I have read a lot of books by now and some have changed my perspective on life but none more than this one. It is said* **'if you seek, so shall you find'**, *but I say 'what shall you find? This book says: 'what are you looking for?' but do I really know?*

I look at my mother, these pigs, my life and question it all. Apparently, according to this book, **'the kingdom of God is within you'** *but what is God? Never mind what is the kingdom of this God?*

He hit several rusty nails into the fence with a large piece of wood and thus connecting two loose pieces of wood together – he had fixed it! He began to ponder again… *it was interesting the way I am able to connect two material objects into one, or seemingly so. I have read of 'transmutation' – a process of turning one thing into another. In this case I have turned two parts of wood into one, whereas from the book I have read, in the world of thought I can turn bad into good.*

This idea that we have a solid physical world and an invisible (or at least to most people) one of thought is intriguing.

From the book he had read he had learnt of the physical, etheric, astral and mental worlds around us and that even these had planes of subdivision.

Having fed the pigs and fixed the fence Pazamor entered the small country house kitchen and sat at the large wooden table ready to eat breakfast.

"Ere ye are Paz, egg and toast!"

Pazamor loved egg and toast, his mother was able to toast the bread to perfection, unlike himself, and the runny egg on top of this was like the morning sun breaking on the day's horizon.

After breakfast Pazamor found himself once again sat on his bed of straw, reading the old book he had once again grabbed from under his pillow, a book which a mysterious elderly man had given him the day before. He read about something called synchronicity… *As I understand this, it means that things in life do not happen by accident, they happen for a reason. Just like meeting that old man yesterday who gave me this book – it feels like this book is really important and is something I need to read and is relevant to my life's journey and self-development at this moment in time and space.*

Pazamor put the book down on the table. Sat at the head of his bed, crossed his legs in a meditative posture, relaxed and expelled his breath. He concentrated on his 'ajna chakra', the point between the eyebrows, and not what is often mistaken by other occultists as the third eye, which is actually behind this chakra point. Within an instant he was at peace and could hear the low buzz of energy around him. He meditated every day after breakfast for about the same length of time it would take him to eat this. His mother thought he was just reading his books and didn't bother him much in his attic sanctuary.

A bell could be heard tolling in the distance – it was now sunrise and judging from the number of rings it was time to leave.

"Paz! It's time for market," shouted Beth, shaking her head as if he should know by now.

Pazamor grabbed his book and rushed down the stairs like a whirlwind. Picking up some bread his mother had made the night before he stuffed a piece into the pocket of his cape and the rest into his sack. He put the book into a special pocket inside his cape, gave his mother a kiss before running to the end of the bumpy, muddy track of a road.

He waited for Farmer Tang to pass by in his horse and cart and waved him down.

"Have ye got payment today Young Paz?"

"Here…" Pazamor passed Tang the loaf of bread from his pocket.

"That'll do fine my boy – thank ye. Climb up," said Farmer Tang offering him his hand. Farmer Tang was an interesting character, while dressed as a typical farmer of the day he looked more like a scarecrow in appearance with bits of straw sticking out of his holey brown leggings and torn chequered jacket, a tooth missing, from drinking too much cider, unkempt brown wind-swept hair, hidden with a battered hat and bushy long eyebrows with wide starring eyes that gave him a crazed look – probably from living on his own for so long.

They continued along the track together. "So Tang, are you happy with life?"

"What Young Paz?" Then something strange happened, it was as if time and space shimmered around Farmer Tang. "Ye be asking me philosophical questions son?"

"I guess," Pazamor was amazed that Tang could speak such a word let alone understand it!"

"Are ye judging me again Young Paz?" questioned Tang, with raised eyebrows.

"Umm … no I should know better Tang," muttered Pazamor sheepishly.

"Quite so Young Paz, quite so! Well then, returning to your question," he said, while stroking his chin in contemplation. "I am a simple person that leads a simple life, I look after my flock well. I feed them when they need feeding," he said this while staring at Pazamor.

Pazamor's cheeks went the colour of beetroot; he felt that Tang was talking about the way he fed his pigs. They always came second to Pazamor's own needs. Farther Tang smiled wryly.

Tang continued… "I rake the earth and sing to the glory of the universe when doing so. If a crop fails, and they do sometimes, then I will try and laugh about it, but keep steady in my *mind's eye* the fact that the next crop will be successful. I do enjoy life Young Paz because happiness is so important, it is not always easy, but it is a necessary part of life, just like the sun is important to my crops, so is happiness important to my soul."

Pazamor listened intently to all that Farmer Tang was saying and thought to never think of him again as a 'country bumpkin!'

"Well here we are son," announced Tang, "I have to see some other people now."

'That was strange', thought Pazamor, Tang was not known for his interaction with others and he was always a bit of a loner. How quickly their journey had passed too.

Pazamor ran to the market square. There were already stalls setting up in the morning sunshine to sell their wares: vegetables, clothes, stones, jewellery and bread! 'Arrh! Someone else was selling bread.' Pazamor approached the stall. A brute of a woman stared at him and noticed the bread he had on him. "Is that for me?" she screamed while trying to grab it from him but missing. "Barrot, get 'im!"

Barrot was a bully of a youth but nearing the age of manhood and built like a prize bull. "Come 'ere titch!" he shouted, "give us ye bread or I'll crush ye!"

Pazamor was slightly older than Barrot and certainly not a 'titch'. He was a lot thinner and lighter and decided to use this to his advantage. Pazamor ran and ran, with Barrot in close pursuit. A short while later however and Barrot had given up the chase.

Pazamor slowed down and began to catch his breath, he hid within an empty, ruined stone building, not visible from the bare, mud path. Some point within this the sun shone inside, catching his attention and bringing him to it. The large stone walls were really thick and the splintered, wooden floor below his feet was broken at points, causing a possible danger if not careful.

He began to think that Barrot would find him and beat him up and then he stopped this train of thought. He remembered the book he had read that stated that *'as we think, so we create'* so instead of seeing Barrot finding him and beating him up he saw Barrot returning to his ogre of a mother.

Pazamor further pondered why Barrot was like this, why he enjoyed hurting others or destroying things. Then Pazamor saw a picture of Barrot's mother in his mind's eye and realised that actually a lot of Barrot came from her – so was she to blame?

Pazamor was too scared to return to the market and kept hidden in the building in which he had found a temporary sanctuary - an old disused church by the looks of things. He stayed for some time looking around and exploring, then finally finding a quiet spot in the wooden tower of the building to meditate, something he normally did at home in the secret confines of his attic space.

As he sat quietly, cross legged on the floor, tears dripped from his eyes as he thought about all the times he had been bullied by Barrot and what he could do about it. It felt like nothing.

Then Pazamor saw in his mind's eye people fighting and he replaced this thought with people throwing down their weapons and hugging each other in peace instead. He saw the dead and dying from wars past and those that had died from disease and starvation. Instead of death he saw their loved ones dressed in white, holding their spirits, as if taking them from their bodies, like a nut from a broken, empty shell, up to an intense white light. Then he saw Barrot standing in front of him in his mind's eye, however he felt no animosity to his foe, instead he saw himself hugging Barrot as a brother – if only!

Then as the pictures faded Pazamor sat quietly in the darkness of his mind and the depths of his soul. His focus of attention dropped, as if to the bottom of his spine and time stood still in total peace, if only for a moment.

Slowly, in the darkness of his mind, a blue circular like outline could be seen. It was like looking up through the shape of the human vertebra, dispersed with space such as each segment of the spine, he could also hear the soft humming or buzzing noise so often heard in his morning meditations. It felt as if he was moving up through these hoops that also vibrated slowly in the darkness. Then it got faster, and more of these faintly coloured blue shapes could be seen, as if moving up through a tunnel, ever faster. The speed of travel increased and increased. Pazamor could feel a slight fear creeping in, he was travelling at a speed faster than anything he knew and the blue shapes were now mere flashes of light, a blur – he could not stop!

His mind's eye was out of control. The serpent had been unleashed but could not be recalled, springing forth as if with the force of a fired arrow from a bow. He reminded himself that he was protected by the ever loving Universal Spirit.

Then it stopped as suddenly as it had begun. Now it felt as if he was above the earth, as if he had stopped on a plateau, there was very little light here, about the same as you can see when you close your eyes. Pazamor calmed and the fear left him. Instead he was now feeling adventurous again. Where was he? What was happening? Then he felt as if two great spiritual beings were watching him, as if surprised to see him, as if he should not be in this domain, at least not yet, not at this time.

BANG! A massive expansion of consciousness took place. He was like a droplet of water splashing into a still pond and as the ripples spread from the centre of the drop so did his consciousness spread to the confines of the universe, to the very edge of the 'ring pass not'. This experience felt like it lasted for but a short time. Pazamor WAS the universe for this time and totally immersed in a fantastic, bright, white light, like none he had ever seen or felt before.

Suddenly he opened his eyes. He was back in the wooden tower, the sunlight playing on his face. His forehead had a cool breeze to it, as if touched by steel. He heard the words with his spiritual ears as clearly as if someone had spoken them – **'In all we are ONE and in one we are whole'.** He sat cross-legged a little longer in the stillness and peace that surrounded him.

Then he jumped up. He still had to sell his bread - but didn't fancy returning to the market and possible conflict with Barrot. He walked down the broken steps of the tower.

What could he do **"Ask and ye shall receive."** He heard someone say aloud. It was Tang, or was it? A figure emerged from the ruins of the building near the entrance.

"Is that you Tang?" asked Pazamor.

"What do you think son?" said Tang. Pazamor looked closely, he looked like Tang, but still something was different, he just couldn't put his finger on what it might be.

"So Young Paz You would seek something more than this life would ye?"

"Sorry?" said Pazamor.

"You heard what I said; you seek something beyond this physical plane?"

"Wait a minute. I know you," said Pazamor. "You are the old man who gave me this book! But you look like Tang."

"Yes, you are right. I have taken Tang's earthly form but I am not Tang, my life force is very different and yes I am the same being that gave you the book in your pocket."

"What are you then?"

"I am a Master, Young Paz and you are my apprentice, one of many."

Pazamor listened intently "A Master – a real live Master?" he said eagerly.

"Are you deaf Young Paz? Yes, I can hide it no longer from your mind's eye. You have taken the first initiation and passed. You will have access to my help in this life and others', however; I will also expect help from you. Do we have a deal?"

"I guess we do Tang," said Pazamor, shaking each other's wrists strongly, in an act of kinship.

Something fell behind Pazamor, he turned to see a termite eaten branch that had fallen from a large dead tree and he heard in his mind *that's an agreement*. He turned again to see that Tang was no longer there. He looked around but could not even find foot prints showing the direction Tang might have taken.

He pondered back to the book: *an 'agreement' is when life around you reacts in such a way as to answer questions asked, by some form of noise or movement at the exact time of questioning – this may seem to occur as if by coincidence.* However, to an occultist, such as Pazamor, there is no such thing as coincidence. Everything has an action and reaction.

This was all very interesting but what about selling the bread? Pazamor plucked up the courage to return to the market square. He had to sell the bread his mother had given him or he would be in serious trouble. As he walked back to town he saw beautiful flowers, hundreds of daises in the grass like bright stars in the night sky, the flowing clouds on the horizon and the birds of the air. Everything around him seemed so much more real! He could still feel the cool breeze in his forehead and was at peace with all around him.

As he continued walking Pazamor did not stop to think that Barrot could still be in the market.

Chapter 2
The Hall of Learning

Pazamor jogged down a muddy slope to the village square. He could clearly see Barrot's mother selling bread to some of his own customers. Pazamor carefully skirted around the edge of the village so as not to bring attention to himself. He could just make out the prices – ten danks each – ouch! He only sold them for six!

He heard the bell toll from the local church – it was now midday, the market was finished and he had not even sold one piece of bread. He could see the stalls packing up – those that had been there paid five danks each to the collector. This middle aged man with silver hair was richly dressed and kept the money securely around his belt, hidden by a purple velvet shirt. Pazamor continued to walk in the direction of the collector. The road he was taking would mean that they would cross paths at some point.

Silly thoughts crossed his mind 'what if he grabbed the bag from the collector? He would certainly have enough money to pay the rent then?' But no, Pazamor was not built that way and understood the universal law of 'karma' only too well. He would surely be caught and punished and it did not fit with how he tried to live life, namely: **'treat others as you would like yourself treated'**.

He thought back to his book and remembered, 'Karma' – **'As you sow, so shall ye reap'**. *I have always found this universal law unwavering in its detail and delivery –* **'he who lives by the sword dies by the sword'***- like my father in the Devian War. Why did he have to die? Was it his karma? He had killed many trolls in his time and he was killed by one such being while on patrol in Black Vintigan Forrest.'*

"Hello Paz," said the collector as they met, waking Pazamor from his thoughts, "you are not trading today?"

"Umm, no Sir."

"But what of your bread?" pointing to Pazamor's sack, in which bread was clearly visible.

The collector was staring at Pazamor's forehead intently.

"I'll tell you what Paz I need a job completing tomorrow," the collector knew that Pazamor needed the money – "I will give you forty danks for this job twenty now and the other twenty on completion."

"That sounds good Sir – but what would you have me do?"

"Meet me by the old south tin mine tomorrow at sunrise and I will explain more to you then."

Pazamor continued home on the worn track, a shortcut home, where he met an old deranged man, dressed in rags, stinking of drink and sat against a large diseased tree stump.

"Can you spare me some food son?" groaned the old man in a shaky voice. Pazamor looked at the old man and remembered all the bread in his sack.

"Yes, sure," he said. He reached for several pieces and handed them to the beggar and was about to continue on his way when he saw it again, it was as if time and space shimmered around the beggar just like it did with Farmer Tang.

"You look tired, make sure you go to bed early tonight," murmured a voice similar to that of Farmer Tang.

"Sorry?" said Pazamor.

"Are you sure you don't have wax between your ears! Did you not hear me the first time?" he sighed.

"Tang!" gasped Pazamor.

"You apprentices are such hard work. What do you expect a master to appear as? Most of the time we are invisible in your world. Most people walk past us or even through us! If I appeared naked would you see me then? - I guess you would pretend I wasn't there!" laughed Tang.

"So what do you wish me to do Master?"

Tang looked at Pazamor, "Just do your best son."

"WOOF! – WOOF!" barked a dog behind Pazamor, he turned to see a small dog barking at him. When he returned his gaze to the beggar, Tang was gone, only the beggar remained.

Pazamor continued on his way down the winding oak forest path, his feet crunching under some nut shells left discarded by red squirrels. He noticed a wind was gathering and the dog was following him. Then he realised he was after his bread. He was hungry! Pazamor threw him a piece and he saw the space around the dog shimmer and looked at his eyes; they were black as coal. One of his eyes seemed to wink at Pazamor and then he was gone, running off with the bread in his mouth and wagging his tail.

Pazamor laughed to himself.

As he continued along the trail he heard horses galloping towards him and horns being blown. It was the Black Guard, a kind of village protection force, they were after something and they were heading his way.

Then Pazamor froze. It should have been in fear but instead he just felt the cool breeze in his forehead. Running towards him at a blistering pace was a small Wood Troll, the appearance was unmistakable, its skin was a dark brown earthen colour, its teeth the colour of ash, its nose, arms and legs were like the twigs and branches of a tree. Its clothes were ragged and torn and it grunted like an animal as it ran. It saw Pazamor but was less interested in him than getting away from the pursuing soldiers. Instead of attacking him it dived just in front of him and hid behind a large fallen tree beside the path.

Something kept Pazamor's sight on what was ahead of him. Four riders in full black battle armour appeared. This was the Black Guard, the same guard his father had been in. Three of them raced past him, while one stopped to quiz him.

"Have you seen a troll pass through here?" he said in a gruff voice.

"Yes. He ran on behind me," but instead of pointing to the tree behind him Pazamor pointed past this, as if to infer the troll was much further along the path.

"Thanks!" said the guard and cantered off along the path in the direction of the other riders.

Suddenly it was quiet again, even the wind dropped. What had Pazamor done? Trolls were known killers of people as well as animal livestock and there was one of them just behind this fallen tree!

Pazamor approached carefully, half expecting the troll to jump out at any minute and attack him. He slowly looked behind the fallen tree. The troll was scared, it even seemed to be crying; green pus falling from its eyes. It stared at Pazamor and realised that actually, Pazamor had protected him. Pazamor lent down towards the troll slowly. He noticed he was pierced, an arrow hung from his side and green liquid oozed from the wound.

Pazamor took the last piece of bread from his pack and gave it to the troll. At first the troll hesitated and then snatched the bread, quickly devouring it.

It nodded to Pazamor, as if to say thank you. The troll passed Pazamor a small, muddy rock it took from its mouth, as if regurgitating it and then bounded out of view into the depths of the forest, soon disappearing from view within the deep undergrowth.

Pazamor continued on his way and was soon home again.

"You're very late Paz. Did ye have any problems today? Did ye sell the bread ok?"

'The bread – oh heck,' thought Pazamor, 'what am I going to tell my mother. He began to rub the muddy stone the troll had given him, worrying about what to tell his mother.

"I gave all the bread away to those in need mother."

"That's good Paz but how much did we make today? I need ta pay the collector his rent."

Pazamor grabbed the twenty danks from his pocket and gave it to her.

"This is good Paz, we just about have enough money for the collector for the next rent payment."

"I also got this stone." He held up what had been a muddy stone, which had now been cleaned by the movement of his hands – both of them stared in awe. The sun's rays caught it and it glittered, sending green shades all around the house in a sparkling radiance.

"An emerald!" they both said in disbelief.

The troll had given Pazamor a prized possession.

"It must be worth at least 3,000 danks!" she murmured.

"Can I give the market a miss for the rest of the week mother?"

She continued to stare at the beauty of the stone.

"How did you get it Paz?"

Pazamor was not lying when he said he had swapped it for bread with a special customer.

"Can I have the rest of the week off then mother? I'm really tired."

Beth continued to stare at the beauty of the stone.

"Yes of course love, of course, but can you try and sell the stone tomorrow?"

"I will try."

Pazamor put the stone in one of his many secret pockets and ran up to the attic, he threw off his sack and jumped onto his bed. He could hear the village bell striking in the distance but he was too tired to take much more notice of anything else around him and he dropped off to sleep.

As he went into a deep sleep he began to think of all the things he had done that day.

Then he was thinking of nothing and was at peace in the darkness of his mind.

The darkness got a little lighter and Pazamor literally awoke within the dream, finding himself at the bottom of a large mountain-like temple, at night and surrounded by what seemed to be a flat desert of sand and very little else. He was on a plateau at the base of this mountain but he could clearly see a large cave-like opening, which was some ten men high directly above him. There were no steps to this opening and no rope. It was a slippery cold surface and un-climbable by man or beast. In fact there was no other visible way of entering this sacred domain.

"Hello," a soft female voice came from behind him, as he was staring at awe at the sight of the mountain-like temple structure.

The voice made him start and he quickly turned around. Before him was a beautiful tall, young lady with long golden flowing hair and bright blue eyes, dressed in a dark blue cloak – but how did she get here?

"Hi!" said another voice. Again Pazamor turned around, to see a young man of similar build and dress. "My name is 'Duke'," he spoke in an aristocratic tone.

"And I am Sapphira," replied the lady.

"I am Pazamor. What is this place?"

"First time here Pazamor?" asked Duke.

"This is the Hall of Learning," replied Sapphira, "we must enter through there to begin our training." She motioned her eyes to the entrance above.

Then it dawned on Pazamor, these people were apprentices too!

Duke sat down in a meditative posture and wasted no time in quickly levitating to the entrance of the temple cave above. He then disappeared within.

"Come on Pazamor, you have flown in your dreams before or you would not be here now. Try," said Sapphira. She began to rise to the entrance while standing and as she did so Pazamor concentrated on making himself feel light and able to fly. Then he also began to rise. He followed Sapphira into the cave-like entrance and also met with Duke again. They both welcomed him with a smile and a touch on each shoulder of his brown cloak – their touch was real.

Ahead of them on the walls were fiery shimmering lights; flaming torches carefully spaced to light the way ahead. The floor turned from stone to wood and creaked under their weight as they walked ahead deeper into the mountain.

Soon they reached a crossroads in the cave's corridor. "Pazamor we have to go to this room, but you are only a novice and must go to the other, along that corridor."

Sapphira pointed further down the corridor to the left. Sapphira and Duke stood before a large heavy wooden door with studs in it. However, they did not open it but instead directly walked through, as ghosts might penetrate a solid wall.

Pazamor stared in disbelief at what he had just seen. He touched the door Sapphira and Duke had seemed to pass through. It was solid wood, with blunt shiny iron studs to reinforce it. He tried to find a handle, but could find none. It was solid and would not budge and there was no lock for a key either.

Pazamor thought to knock on the door but instead continued in the direction given by Sapphira.

He could hear chanting coming from ahead. As he turned the corner he saw twelve people dressed in simple brown gowns, the same clothes as worn by holy men. They were kneeling before a wall, chanting gently. One of these motioned Pazamor to approach and sit with them. Pazamor knelt at the back of the group and also began to chant.

OM… OM… OM… they sounded in a deep tone that vibrated throughout the temple walls. His body and the sound merged as one.

*

"Dong, Dong, Dong, Dong, Dong, Dong…"
Pazamor awoke.

It was time to rise, he had certainly slept well! But wait, he had agreed to meet the collector early today. He would have to run!

He opened the attic door and ran down the stairs and rushed outside the back of the house to feed the pigs in the usual way. Throwing the sludge of food into the trough, he stepped back, but as he was not fully concentrating he failed to observe a tiny pig behind him.

"Oink! Oink!" It blasted past to get to the trough. Pazamor was knocked flying and ended up in the mud, at least that's what he hoped it was!

He slowly got up. It was horrible and sticky but rather than curse he laughed his head off, dusted off what he could and proceeded to the hens' pen.

He lifted the first hen to see if there were any eggs: one light brown and white spotted egg. However, the second hen had been watching and was ready ... peck, peck it stabbed at Pazamor's hand.

"Ouch!" He pulled back his hand quickly. They both stared at each other. But the hen was having none of it. Pazamor was not going to rudely lift her and take her egg. It was hers!

Pazamor tried again, but with the same reaction. "Ouch!"

He stopped to reflect. He only really needed one egg for his mother as today he did not have time to eat breakfast himself, if he was to get to the south mines in time.

He left the other hen alone and she clucked as if she had gained a victory over him.

Pazamor may have lost this battle but he would certainly win the war. He would get the egg tomorrow he thought.

He took the egg he had managed to retrieve into the house and put it in his mother's small metal pot with the wooden handle.

He grabbed his sack from the loft and a small piece of bread she had left for him on the table.

It must be getting late by now, he thought as he rushed along. He pondered back to his book... *'Move slowly in life if you wish to move quickly'. What was that all about? He would be late if he did not run very fast today.* While he was thinking this and running along he saw Farmer Tang. He was very early today, thought Pazamor.

"Ye seem in a rush Young Paz. Do ye need a lift?"

"That would be of help Tang," said Pazamor jumping up.

"Ufff... what is that smell?" even the horse seemed to turn its head in distaste.

"Oh sorry, I had an accident."

"An accident! Did you forget to use the large leaves placed by the whole in your field?" said Tang laughing.

"You need to look after these bodies of yours – try cleaning yourself with water!" he said with that wry smile.

Pazamor laughed. He was speaking to the Master again.

"So, how did you get on in the Hall of Learning?"

Pazamor thought for a moment at what Tang could be talking about and then vaguely remembered his dream the night before.

"Oh that was a great dream he said"

"Was it a dream Young Paz?"

Pazamor looked at Tang. "Are you saying it was real?"

"You need to recognise the real from the unreal Young Paz.

Today you will have a big test ahead of you. Remember that if you get stuck just ask and I can be there. But do try every other avenue first as it is not good to rely on others to the extent that they do all the work for you." Pazamor remembered what he had read in his book ... **'It is better to give than to receive'**, especially if given with love.

They got to the South Mines just on time. Pazamor could see the collector near a wooden shack.

"Bye then Paz," said Tang, as he left the way he had come.

"Thanks," said Pazamor waving.

"Hello there Paz.   Are you ready for today's challenge?" smiled the collector.

"I guess I am Sir."

"Well, up ahead is the entrance to the disused old South Tin Mine and in there lives a Cave Troll that owes me money – namely eighty danks. Please give him this chit to remind him."   The collector handed Pazamor a piece of parchment which had the mark of a troll and against this the danks owed. He also handed Pazamor a lighted torch.

Cave Trolls were not the friendliest of creatures on a good day and handing the chit to one might enrage it.   Still Pazamor had now agreed to the job, having had half the payment.

He entered the dark cave pushing large cobwebs out of the way with the lighted torch in hand, which spluttered with some of the gas residues. He knew he would have to go down very deep to find the troll. Sometime later and he still could not find the troll in question and the torch's light was getting low.

He looked on the walls for any spare torches as he continued down the mine, but the ones he found were spent.

Then he heard a loud roar in the distance. It must be the Cave Troll he thought. It could probably hear him. Though slow and heavy, Cave Trolls were very strong and had excellent hearing.

Pazamor crept deeper into the cave, he could hear the loud footsteps approaching and getting closer.

The very ground shook as the troll came into view. This was a big one! Its skin matched the dark walls of the cave and if it was to stand still it would have been very well camouflaged.

The troll was only a few paces away now and its dull red eyes could clearly be seen, along with its massive muscular arms and sturdily built body. Pazamor's body froze and could not find the power to move forward a step closer.

The troll let out a deafening roar, as loud as a fully grown lion. It was not happy with the intrusion, into what it regarded as its home.

Pazamor lifted the chit in front of him. The troll was now at arm's reach and snatched the chit. He moved his head back and forth, closely examining the symbols. He roared again and destroyed the chit, crumpling and crushing it into tiny pieces. He shook a large fist at Pazamor in anger.

Pazamor took a step back to avoid a possible hit from his clenched knuckles. Then it all went dark. The torch he had been holding had spluttered out. "God help me!" thought Pazamor, then he heard in his head 'the stone, the stone' and in his mind's eye he pictured the green stone.

Pazamor instinctively grabbed the small stone from his pocket and held it out. It gave out a dull glow that enabled him to see the outline of the troll. The troll stopped in its tracks and let out a noise that sounded like a gasp. It dropped to its knees trying to hide its eyes from the stone's light.

"The money please," said Pazamor. The troll was now the one edging back and trying to avoid the green glow of the stone that Pazamor held up in front of him.

The Cave Troll turned its back on Pazamor. It regurgitated something in a similar manner to the Wood Troll, and then spun around to present Pazamor with a giant bar of tin ore, interspaced with what looked like gold flakes. While passing this to Pazamor with one hand it covered its eyes with the other.

Pazamor took the metal bar with one hand, as he was still holding the green stone with the other. He could not hold it for long as the weight of the metal was too great. It fell to the ground with a thud!

The troll ran off in the direction it had come.

Pazamor put the green stone down on the floor and placed the tin ore in his sack. Picking up the stone again, he struggled with the weight to make his way back to the surface, the green stone dimly lighting his way.

As he travelled up towards the exit he looked more closely at the stone and could make out a troll-like symbol, though he was not sure what it meant.

Eventually he reached the surface to find the collector, who was surprised to see Pazamor so quickly.

"Any luck Young Paz?"

"I did get something for my trouble," said Pazamor panting for breath.

Pazamor dropped his sack to the ground. The ore of tin and gold was fully visible, as the sack opened.

The collector's eyes widened and a smile broke out on his face. "Well done Young Paz. This will clear the troll's debt and here is your other twenty danks.

"Can you read Troll Sir?"

"Yes, and write it Young Paz."

"Can you read this symbol for me," said Pazamor holding up the stone and showing the collector the symbol on it.

"This is no ordinary stone Young Paz, it is a 'lode' stone, magical by your definition, and the mark is ancient Deva not Troll. It is these stones that were used as weapons against us humans in the Devian War by the Cleric Wood Trolls. How did you come by it?"

"A Wood Troll I helped gave it to me."

"That would not be enough to give you such a valuable item, though used as a weapon by these people it can also be used for peace. In a similar way, a sword can be used defensively or it can be used to attack, so can this stone be utilised for good or bad. This troll must have recognised good in you or the mark of the apprentice..." the collector paused. 'I thought as much,' he pondered.

Pazamor was fascinated by what he had heard.

"You need to talk to Abbot Tarock from the Celthina Monastery, he can guide you further."

Pazamor had heard of this place but only knew it to be to the north.

Chapter 3
The Celthina Monastery

This ancient monastery was set on a hillside away from any large villages, remote from people or marauding bands of trolls and protected by a massive surrounding wall, some ten men high.

One tower within it was most impressive, at over twenty men high it was the tallest building in the land.

It had a network of buildings interlinked and made of red and orange stone that glowed like the sun when it set in the evening sky.

A large mirror set in the tower would send out a signal that the day was ending and the night was beginning in worship to the Universal Spirit. It was said that the ancients had made the tower and surrounding monastery by the use of sound, a technology which was said to have been long lost.

Abbot Tarock was the chief monk in charge of the monastery and he was very hard to reach at the best of times. He was a well built man, more like a warrior than a monk. He had long black hair but with the distinct bald hole cut in the middle, a jagged scar down the left side of his face across the eye where a sword had hit long ago. It was said he had been in the Devian War and was one of the few to have survived.

Before leaving on this journey, Pazamor had given his mother the money from the collector, explained were he was travelling to and that he would be gone for a while. He had managed to grab an egg, some bread and a flagon of water. The collector had also given Pazamor a rough map he had drawn for him of Dronagon's Domain with the monastery on it. Pazamor had the stars and his father's compass to help guide him.

*

After travelling for half a day, Pazamor was getting tired. Making a small fire near a fast running stream, and using the lid of his flagon he collected some water, to boil the egg within while he toasted some bread on a stick. He sat down on a large rock nearby to eat and after filling himself took out his book and began to read:

'When you meditate pick a quiet spot, ideally somewhere undisturbed and a place you can use regularly. You do not need to sit in any special posture, even a good chair will do but keep your back straight and your muscles relaxed. Concentrate on the ajna chakra and keep your concentration there.

However, a word of warning everything must be in moderation and you must balance your life, overdo nothing, least you put your life force at risk. Live a life of service which helps ground the spiritual energies gained from meditation. Service can be giving healing but on a truly divine level it is most simply helping others unconditionally from the heart.' As he continued to read the book he could feel the cool breeze in his ajna chakra. Pazamor further pondered... *Have I found myself through meditation? If I take a microscope and continually increase the magnification looking at ever smaller things or if I take a telescope and look ever deeper into space and planets ever further away - when will I see that a tiny atom is the same as planet, in that both are living organisms – when will the two meet up and come full circle?'*

Pazamor heard a rustle from some thorn bushes behind him. He stared up to see a rabbit rush by. He drank the water from the flagon's glass lid, which had now cooled enough to drink and kicking out the remains of his camp fire put the book and flagon away, grabbed his sack and continued on his way.

Using his map and compass, he continued north along the river as he had been instructed by the collector.

While trolls could live here, Pazamor tried not to think too much of this. He believed that he was protected and that was enough for him, besides he loved and respected nature and was sure that Wood Trolls appreciated such things too.

He admired the beauty of the trees and the calming sound of the rushing river, turned white by the rapids. Then he saw some fish darting away from his shadow. He had no net with him but had an idea to catch some. He continued along the river until he found an area that opened up, it was slightly deeper than the rest of the river and slower moving. Pazamor hunted around for the largest flattest stone he could find. When he found it he brought it to the edge and stood so that his shadow was not cast on the water but the pebbled beach instead.

As he waited he could see several fish coming down the river, he slowly lifted the stone and waited. As they came closer he threw the large stone directly at them. SPLASH! The water was thrown up into the air getting Pazamor a little wet in the process. Three small fish the size of a hand were now on the beach beside him. He managed to grab two of them before they could flip back into the river, the other escaping before he could grab it.

Knocking them hard against the rocks he killed them instantly. He then found some large leaves to wrap the fish and placed them in his sack. He thanked the universe for the food it had provided him.

After a long time travelling the sun was starting to set and it began to get dark. He would have to set up camp for the night very soon and began to look for the best place to do this as he continued on his journey.

He noticed a small concave outline within the river bank. It offered some protection from the elements and would be perfect to build a fire safely without catching the forest alight, something which would not be a good idea!

Pazamor took some hay from his sack, twigs and branches from the forest floor and built a small fire to cook the freshly caught fish. He lit the fire by rubbing a long stick very fast between his hands on another piece of wood, the friction causing heat, and sparks which were enough to light the fire.

He built a spit for the fish, skewering them with this, and placing them over the fire. He sat cross legged and grabbed his little book to read in the fading light:

'When you meditate in the same undisturbed space over a period of time you generate a sound and an aura that are like a protecting shell. This offers you some protection from

forces that might steal your energy and enables you to better meditate. Meditation is essentially the art of linking the physical with the spiritual while still alive in the body. It gives the soul the chance to grab the physical vehicle, energise it and hopefully utilise it in worthy service.

After about forty days of daily meditations it becomes possible to see these auras surrounding all life forms.'

Pazamor put the book down and pondered. The light from the sun was very low now. He calmly sat in a meditative posture and slowly looked around. He could see none of the auras mentioned in the book. But wait, there was a dark soft blue outline around his sack. He looked at his arm as he slowly moved it across his body while keeping his head still and could also see this blue/white outline following behind the movement of his arm.

'Hummn… what was that burning smell.' Sniff! Sniff! 'The fish!' Pazamor grabbed them quickly from the fire burning his hand in the process. "Ouch!" he shouted.

He quickly ran to the river to cool his hands but instead tripped over his cape as he bent over and went tumbling into the river with a great SPLASH!

He struggled to get up when he saw someone rushing towards him. A young, tall man, slightly older than Pazamor, offered him a hand and Pazamor grabbed it jumping out just as quickly as he had fallen in - the water was freezing!

He was so soaked to the skin that he forgot about his burnt hand.

"It's f-f-f-f freezzzzing!" he said.

They both laughed aloud.

"Hello, my name is Duke. What is yours?"

They both looked at each other for a while, as if they had met before, but were not sure where.

"I am Pazamor. Would you like some burnt fish?"

The both laughed again.

"Yes, that would be good I have not had some for a few sunrises now," smiled Duke.

"What are you doing here," they both said at the same time. They laughed again.

"You first," said Pazamor.

"I am on my way to see the Abbot."

"Me too!" said Pazamor.

They shared the fish and a little bread together.

Pazamor had taken off the wet cloths and Duke had given him his richly made cape, which was much thicker than Pazamor's, to keep warm, while his clothes dried near the fire.

They looked at the stars as the sun disappeared and moved closer to the warmth of the fire, exchanging stories and sharing some of Duke's biscuits from their remaining provisions. Sat under the starry night sky Pazamor got changed again into some of the clothes which had now dried.

Duke put a few more branches on the fire and they both fell into a deep sleep.

*

The next day they awoke early. Duke got up first and went to rebuild the fire; he dug it around and managed to find an old ember still alight. While he played with the fire, Pazamor sat to meditate quietly.

Duke carefully blew the embers until the fire lighted up. He took some twigs already collected the night before and placed them over the embers. He was better at building fires than Pazamor and probably better at travelling also.

Pazamor was already missing his bed at home.

As Pazamor sat meditating on his ajna chakra he felt the cold breeze *in* his forehead. Some moments later he could see a bright white light in front of his mind's eye and he merged with this. It was so peaceful. He slowly opened his eyes, he could feel them rolling down from his head to their normal position. As he did this he could still feel the cool breeze across his forehead.

In front of him sat Duke cooking what looked like wild mushrooms with nuts for breakfast.

"Smells good Duke," said Pazamor, sniffing the air.

"Yes, I learnt this from my gran, Pazamor."

"You can call me Paz, Duke, all my friends do."

They crunched on the nuts and chewed on the mushrooms, while sipping some boiled water.

"How long have you been meditating Paz?" asked Duke.

"About one summer. How about you?"

"Oh, about two summers," said Duke with a smile.

They both got along well, as if they had known each other for a very long time.

Duke stood up and adjusted his belt. It was then that Pazamor realised he was wearing light armour and had a short sword by his side.

We better get moving Paz. It is still a good day's travel to the Celthina Monastery and our meeting with Abbot Tarock.

As they left together it felt more like a march. Duke was very fit and acted like a knight in every way. He came across as bold, fearless and well educated.

As they marched on, Pazamor found himself stumbling a few times in order to keep up.

After half a day's travel they could now see the way ahead in the dim distance, from the vantage point of a small hill they had climbed. Standing tall to the north was the

Celthina Tower, but it looked like a small twig from this distance.

They were about to climb down the hill when Duke noticed dust being thrown up from the east and seemingly heading towards the monastery.

"What is that?" asked Pazamor in a surprised tone, pointing to what they both saw ahead.

"It looks like a band of warriors – probably 200 strong, judging by the dust. They have come from the direction of Fort Nomad."

They both looked in that direction. A thick cloud of black smoke could be seen coming from the fort.

"Are they good or bad?" gasped Pazamor in a concerned tone.

"I can't tell Paz. But I feel we must reach the monastery before they do."

They both jogged ahead towards their shared goal, pacing themselves as best they could in the hope they would reach the monastery before the warriors they had spied.

As they ran they tried to hold a conversation.

"Paz do not think that we will not get there on time, but rather that we will. We need to project in our mind's eye that we will get there before the warriors and that we will be safe."

"I understand Duke. We must remain positive in everything that we do."

"Exactly!"

Time passed and they had made good ground but Pazamor was clearly not used to the pace and was already tired.

"I need to rest Duke!" gasped Pazamor.

"No!" said Duke, "our lives may well depend on this, you must push yourself and we must keep going."

They continued but Pazamor was now near collapsing and even Duke was tiring. They could see the walls of the monastery and the tower was much clearer but they were still a distance away.

Nothing could be seen of the warriors crossing the open desert.

Unbeknown to Pazamor and Duke these warriors were now nearing the forested area the same part that Pazamor and Duke were about to enter.

Pazamor and Duke slowed down and rested against a large tree. Duke decided to climb it to gain a vantage point and find out where they were in relation to the warriors.

"I can't see them Paz, where are they?" spoke Duke in a concerned tone.

"Well Duke, we must assume they have gone another route and we will get to the monastery first."

They both laughed but it was an uneasy laugh.

As they lacked the energy to run they marched instead. Building up a rhythm together, walking side by side as quickly as they could but without using as much energy as running, they continued to make good progress towards the monastery.

They were still some distance away. However, to the east they could now see blacker smoke rising. The warriors were about the same distance of travel to the monastery as themselves.

The sun was getting low in the sky, and even though far away, chanting could be heard coming from the monastery. From the tower the great mirror reflected the last rays of light to tell of the day ending and the night approaching.

The chanting vibrated through the whole forest OM, OM, OM…

Duke and Pazamor had no choice but to find somewhere to sleep for the night as they would not be admitted into the monastery at this time. No one would.

Chapter 4
The Art of Dreaming

The morning came and both Duke and Pazamor were still tired and hungry from the day before, neither having slept well. Duke again climbed a tree to see what lay before them.

The monastery itself was but a short distance now and clearly visible. However, he could see no further activity near it or from the east where they had seen smoke rising the day before.

"We need to approach the monastery with stealth, Paz. None must see us, least of all the possible marauders from the east."

They both grabbed their things and started off on their travels again, this time at a more sedate pace than the day before.

By midday they had reached their destination, the forest having slowed their approach.

Pazamor stared in awe at the site that met them as the forest cleared, and before them was the Celthian Monastery.

Pazamor had heard of it but never seen it this close before in all its glory.

The wall of stone that surrounded it was thicker and taller than any castle in the land and its distinct orange stonework masterly crafted. It was said to have been constructed by dwarves, over four Centuries ago, when they and man were friendlier to each other.   [Dwarves were also known to be expert blacksmiths as well as superb craftsman and builders.]

Both walked closer towards the main entrance, a large gatehouse, built in the classic style of castles for that time.

A small aperture the size of a hand opened within the main door, and a voice enquired their business.

"We have both come to see the Abbot," said Duke eagerly.

"Many people come to see the Abbot. Who sent you?"

"We have been sent by the Master T," responded Pazamor.

There was a pause, and they could hear the person they spoke to walk off in the distance and then in front of them a small door opened within the large gate to enable them to pass through.

Pazamor looked around to see substantial defences above and below him: a roof that had holes in it for spears to be thrust through, slits in the walls for archers and the wooden floor had a strangely distinctive cut in the middle; suggesting it could be dropped at any time and anyone standing on it would slip below to an unknown fate.

As they approached a large portcullis, the same person appeared again behind this, and as the door behind them closed by itself, the one in front of them began to rise.

"Hello. I am Benedict but you can call me Brother."

"Greetings Brother," said Duke.

"Hello," said Pazamor sheepishly.

"You will have to work to our rules while within these walls, if you cannot abide by our rules then you must leave – this is our way. The monks are working at this time of the day and it is the best time to catch Abbot Tarock. I will take you to him."

They strolled through a large open courtyard that was tremendously green and beautiful with well tended trees and flowers. To their left monks were working on what looked like a herb and vegetable garden, with other crops like corn and wheat visible in the distance, while to the right were penned animals: goats, a cow, geese and hens. There was even a large pond stocked with fish and a bridge that extended over it. A stone well also stood nearby and must have been extremely deep to collect water from this high altitude.

There were many stone seats around the complex and some monks were sitting in silence on these as if praying or meditating.

They passed one small open building in which some monks sat observing what looked like a teacher speaking in another language. In another section of the abbey monks were making very slow perfectly synchronised bodily movements with their arms and legs.

Further on from this was a smaller group of monks fighting with long staffs. They were expert fighters in defence and blistering fast.

They reached a long two story stone building in which some steps on the outside led up to the first floor. Through the door could be seen a monk seated by the window, writing on a large parchment with a quill pen made from a goose feather copying an ancient symbol from an open scroll. When he saw Duke and Pazamor enter the room he dropped the quill and grabbed Duke around the waist, lifting him off the ground and shouting, "Welcome friend!" in a strong voice.

They both had large smiles on their faces, the type of smile that comes from the heart, clearly displaying that they knew each other well but had not seen each other for a long time.

"Come into my private study friends," said Abbot Tarock, "you too Benedict."

As they sat they could not help but admire the large range of scrolls Abbot Tarock had.

"So what is up my friend?" asked Tarock looking at Duke.

"I do not know fully except our Master told me to see you here and that I would meet with two others and that together we would be responsible for helping this land and its people enormously."

"Well I have had heard rumours that Lord Kraytos has taken King Dronagon captive. That the king is virtually under house arrest in his own castle at Dragon's Teeth Mountain and that Lord Kraytos has an eye to rule this Kingdom by any means necessary."

"That blasted wizard Torrum is behind this with his meddling Duke! Through some accident of his magic and meddling with nature he has created an army of demons and they are under the control of Lord Kraytos, one that practises the dark arts. Someone called Sapphira knows the full story. She is a wizard from Wizards Way, she will be the fourth member you seek in your party."

"Did you know that Fort Nomad looks as if it has been attacked? We saw black smoke coming from it and what looked like 200 warriors, with many on horseback approaching in this direction," whispered Duke.

"This is bad news Duke you will not have enough time to meet up with Sapphira from Wizard's Way in the physical. You must instead continue to Fort Nomad on a perilous mission."

A bell was heard to clang from the main church building within the monastery – it was time for midday prayer.

"You must accompany me to worship – after which you may eat and Brother Benedict will assist you further in your mission."

They entered the main hall with all the other monks. Everyone took a seat in the wooden pews facing the main alter. Abbot Tarock stood behind the main alter to address everyone and spoke in a loud deep voice:

"Brothers, a time could be approaching when we may have to fight again, not to attack but to defend. You know our ways do not permit us to kill unless we ourselves are threatened – well I fear that dark time is with us again. To the east of us has been sighted a small army. They have been seen pulling down trees and making siege devices. I can only conclude that they wish to use these against us – we must be ready if they do."

"We have heard that our king has been captured by a Lord with the name of Kraytos, a wizard of the black arts.

We must remember that we are of the light and that we are stronger than the darkness. That if there should be any war with light and darkness then my dear brothers – we shall win."

All the monks sounded out: "OM …. OM … OM…" Pazamor found himself also doing this and was surprised to feel the power of that word. So deep was it that it felt like it came from somewhere more than just the mouth. The whole of the building vibrated with the sound, some of the OM's were longer and louder than others. Each built on the last getting louder than the first in succession.

After a while they stopped. There was complete silence and peace. Then a bell rang again. They all said together, "Praise be to the universe." All rose and left for the Great Hall, a finely decorated hall with marble pillars and floor, buttressed walls and ornate windows – a place they would all eat.

Pazamor was about to ask Duke a question when Duke put his finger over his lips as if to say, 'quiet do not speak here'.

All the monks had large chalice-like wooden cups filled with water and deep wooden bowls filled with a mixture of cheese, grapes and bread they had produced themselves within the confines of the monastery – they were totally self-sufficient.

They all ate very, very slowly and in total peace. Pazamor was a bit embarrassed; he had half finished his food to see that Duke, sitting next to him, was still on his first grape!

Pazamor too began to slow down and while eating some bread when he would have normally wolfed it down, stopped and just kept chewing it very slowly. He kept chewing the same piece until it began to taste strange, even sugary and noticed that he was very relaxed in himself.

Normally after such a meal, eaten in haste, he would have stomach ache but now he felt the energy from this food being released.

After all had finished, thanks was given and they left to go back to their work or study.

As they were leaving Duke whispered to Pazamor, "When you eat each mouthful Paz think something positive – like: 'I am assimilating Peace'."

Pazamor, Duke and Benedict left the building with the other monks.

"We need the Halls of Sleep!" said Brother Benedict, in an authoritive tone, not unlike that of Abbot Tarock.

'That sounded strangely familiar!' thought Pazamor. "Do you mean the Hall of Learning?" he asked.

Benedict laughed, "In a way – yes," he said, "though most do not remember these experiences of sleep."

He led them to a small modest stone room with nothing but three elevated stone slabs arranged in a 'Y' shape the headstones at the centre of the stone. They all lay down on the stones, heads almost together. It was a very peaceful room but a little dark, except a small hole in the roof, at which Pazamor stared.

Pazamor could feel that cool breeze again in his forehead while looking at a shaft of light entering the room through the hole and became drowsy.

Soon his body was asleep, but his mind was fully awake.

Again he found himself on a desert plain at the foot of a mountain structure. Duke was already waiting, he saw Benedict appear and then Sapphira.

"Well, now that we are all together, let's go," said Benedict motioning them towards the cave entrance above.

They all held each other's hands and floated up together. After reaching the entrance and entering they travelled on foot along the cave's many corridors. Finally they passed a place Pazamor remembered well. It was the room he had practised chanting the sacred sound.

There was a small door behind this room, hidden by a wall cloth, which Benedict pulled aside and they followed in single file along a smaller, narrow corridor which wound deeper up the mountain side, round and round they went. Though there were no steps, it was clear this was a tower-like structure.

Eventually they came to another door. Benedict sounded a word or note and the door creaked open. They all entered.

A round chamber opened before them, with a round table in the middle.

Thirteen seats of stone were placed around this marble table, with what looked like the moon lighting the room from a large white crystal, the size of a man's head, placed in the roof above.

Sapphira sat at the head seat. It was slightly larger than the rest, they could all see each other clearly.

Benedict started, "Welcome Sister," he said.

"Thank you Benedict," she spoke softly. "I am sorry I cannot be in the physical with you now but I have a pressing story of importance. It starts as such:

There is a wizard by the name of Torrum that lived in Dagmars's Tower, situated in Wizard's Way.

Torrum was seeking the Elixir of Life, busy working away in the peaceful confines of his tower and always trying to do more than one thing at once. He had been experimenting with the tissue of Cave Trolls but found he did not have enough. This was not a problem for a wizard and so he called for a conjurer who fetched the old wizard's book of spells.

Torrum called out a duplication spell from his glowing book, while moving his hands over the dead troll's remains. A minor bird [the main mode of communication between wizards across the lands] which belonged to Lord Kraytos, flew through a loop-hole of the tower and brought with it a message. It flew around the room but was more intent on screeching out the last few lines of the duplication spell over and over again, rather than give the message it had been sent to give.

The conjurer tried to grab it, but it flew higher within the tower's roof.

Then the miner bird swooped onto the table that Torrum had been working on in creating the Elixir, having spotted some bread - Torrum's lunch.

Torrum could not grab the bird as he was buried under masses of dead trolls. The conjurer also tried but was stuck fast to the floor by the masses of bodies now piling up towards the roof of the tower.

The Elixir bottle wobbled as the bird hit the table hard and then rolled onto the floor smashing and as it did exploding into a mist of green smoke

Both Torrum and the conjurer were knocked unconscious by the mysterious mist.

However, when they awoke the Trolls' bodies were all gone and all around Wizard's Way were holes and large tunnels in the ground, were earth had been thrown up, as if some giant animals had buried out of the town."

"Wow," gasped Pazamor, listening intently to the story.

Sapphira continued, "In wizard lore, those that cast the spell own the spell and in this case it is the minor bird that speaks in Kraytos's tongue – hence they will obey Kraytos and no one else. This newly created monster has been called the Kraytos Demon and we, the brotherhood of wizards, have managed to classify and catalogue it.

Soon after, an attack took place on Dronagon Castle and the king was taken prisoner. It is said that Lord Kraytos, who resides in Dagmar's Tower within the castle grounds, seeks control of Dronagan's Domain and will stop at nothing to get rid of those in his path."

"How do you know all this Sapphira?" asked Duke.

"Oh Duke!" she said with a great sigh. "I was there when it happened - I was the conjurer under Torrum's instruction."

"You work for that bumbling old wizard Sapphira?"

Sapphira turned her head in disgust at what Duke had just said.

"Yes, I am now the apprentice of Torrum and he has sent me to help you and Pazamor correct this situation."

Now it was Duke's turn to move his head away in disgust, as if to say none of this would have happened if not for the Wizard Torrum.

"Well friends, how can we stop this Lord Kraytos – any ideas?" asked Benedict.

"What of the Sorcerer's Sword?" asked Duke.

"That was broken up after the Devian War Duke - you know the history as well as any," replied Benedict.

"Yes, that might work," said Sapphira, "but wasn't a part of it placed for protection in Fort Nomad?"

"Indeed it was Sapphira – the blade, if I remember correctly," said Duke.

"What of the other parts?" asked Pazamor.

"The hilt is somewhere in Port Kepland but I do not know where. The gemstone which gives the sword its magic is hidden in Black Vintigan Forest."

"A quest!" said Duke eagerly, holding up his hand in delight.

"Yes!" said Sapphira and Pazamor together.

A bell could be heard in the distance and then Pazamor, Duke and Benedict awoke.

"Keep your thoughts, keep your dreams and remember what you have seen and heard!" said Benedict aloud.

They all looked at each other and discussed what they had seen and experienced before the experience could fade completely from their minds.

The thing that they knew was that they must reach Fort Nomad and try and find the first part of the Sorcerer's Sword before Lord Kraytos – that is, if he had not already done so.

Benedict managed to find three horses, one for Pazamor, one for Duke and one for himself, while he went off to sort out unfinished business and prepare provisions for the short journey ahead.

Pazamor looked on in horror – "A horse!" he gasped.

"Yes, Pazamor it's a horse," laughed Duke.

"No – you don't understand Duke, I have never ridden a horse before!"

"You have to be kidding Paz. Never?"

"Nope!" he moaned.

"Well you better learn now. On foot it will take at least two if not three sunrises to Fort Nomad, but with a horse less than one."

Pazamor used some steps attached to one building created especially for mounting a horse, while Duke just jumped up as if it was second nature.

"Don't pull too hard on the reigns Paz," said Duke.

However, Duke gave the advice a little late as Pazamor had already done this and the horse reared and bolted towards the large lake near the centre of the monastery. Pazamor held on for dear life and shouted "Stop! Stop!" However the horse did not understand him but when it reached the water it did stop and threw Pazamor into the lake with a great SPLASH!

Pazamor quickly jumped out of the water. One of the monks looked disapprovingly at Pazamor. "You need a rod to catch the fish," he said.

Duke galloped over, "You seem to like an evening bathe Paz?" They both laughed.

Duke helped train Pazamor the basics of riding a horse - it took them the rest of the day to complete this task but by the end of it Pazamor understood and had become more accomplished.

When Benedict returned, the bell rang and they had to drop what they were doing to attend the main church again.

After two more tolls of the monastery's bell it was time for 'Lectio Divina' – it was now early evening. He saw the light reflected from the tower and could hear a group of monks sounding out the OM across the land, from this great pinnacle of light.

This was a special time that was perfect for Pazamor to read his book in peace and meditate for a while as well.

He went to the monks' library which could be found in the highest point of the tower and found a quiet room nearby to read. While very basic, the room was white and reflected the candle light well, making this the perfect place to read with ease. Enough candles made reading easy and he could see the sun setting over the land. He could even see his home village in the distance and dreamt a bit of home. He saw his mother briefly in his mind's eye and covered her in golden light to protect her from any unseen dangers.

Then he got out his book and began to read again:

'It is best to remain vegetarian if you wish to raise your vibration. Though you may eat fish, which is neutral, avoid red and white meat as it will bring your rate of spiritual vibration down, grounding you and stopping your spirit from rising to the heights. If you take further steps in cutting out cheese, eggs and milk then it can be possible to see things beyond the physical plane. This can be hard for most and even unnecessary, sometimes affecting the health of the instigator for the worse, but a diet of pure vegetables and water will enable easier astral projection, the seeing of auras and greater healing energy to be given.

A word of warning – one must **'know the real from the unreal':** *choose well.*

The food you eat surely effects the physical temple into which it enters – eat anything with love and peace, cook and share it in the same way and you will raise the vibrations of those who eat it – whatever the type of food.'

Pazamor further pondered – so what was expected of him? Well he loved his cheese and while he did not mind giving up red and white meat (he could never catch it half the time anyway!) he would still keep with fish, eggs, cheese and milk for the while. Yes, he would take this path slowly and in a balanced way.

After the last bell of the day sounding 'compline' all the monks, Pazamor and Duke gathered again in the main church building and sounded **'The Great Invocation'** from memory:

From the point of Light within the mind of God
Let light stream forth into the minds of men.
Let Light descend on Earth.

From the point of Love within the Heart of God
Let love stream forth into the hearts of men.
May Christ return to Earth.

From the centre where the Will of God is known
Let purpose guide the little wills of men
The Purpose which the Masters know and serve.

From the centre which we call the race of men
Let the Plan of Love and Light work out.
And may it seal the door where evil dwells.
Let Light and Love and Power restore the Plan on Earth.

As Pazamor, Duke and Benedict left for bed Pazamor noticed that the steeple of the church was glowing a hazy blue and white. He mentioned it to Duke.

"You have the eye of seeing Paz. That is the group energy created by us all as it is being channelled through the shape of the steeple to where it is needed by the Masters of wisdom into our world. Any building with such a pyramidal shape can be used in this way, as a transmitter. For you and me, the tetrahedron is our shape of power and not this pyramid type. Though the master will still make use of it for good never minding if it is a pyramid or tetrahedron based.

We have called on them to channel these energies by use of The Great Invocation."

They both bid Benedict a good evening and settled down for the night in separate but very small simple rooms with a bed, chair, table and small window slit.

Tomorrow they would ride.

Chapter 5
Dangerous Encounter

They awoke early the next day before the monastery's bell could ring out. Brother Benedict packed their provisions; they mounted their horses and left well before sun rise.

After they had travelled for some time east they could see a faint smoke cloud rising from the forest canopy ahead of them. Duke indicated with his hands to dismount from their horses and stay where they were, while he scouted on ahead.

Pazamor and Benedict tied the horses and kept them under cover. They sat down to talk in quiet whispers.

"The monastery has not been attacked since the Devian War Pazamor. At that time we had some 2,000 trolls attacking, so if this is only 200 we shouldn't have a problem – we are well trained and have excellent defences."

"How many monks did you have defending the monastery at that time Benedict?" asked an intrigued Pazamor.

"We had 500 at that time Pazamor but we had losses also, and to this day we have had difficulty replacing those numbers."

"Why have you had difficulty in replacing your numbers then Benedict?"

"Well, unlike the military profession, we do not press-gang people into service, rather we try to attract them to the spiritual path – we are searching for people that are seeking themselves and wishing to help others. However, in this Dark Age in which we live, most people are getting more selfish and do not care much for the spiritual path, rather they would invest in the physical world instead."

"Are you saying that most people are too busy with life to find out about life?"

"Exactly Pazamor! It is that simple. If people would only seek the Universal Spirit first then everything else would follow, but most are not able to take this leap of faith."

Time and space shimmered around Benedict and then he spoke in a different tone, that of Tang:

"Did you know that the trolls were once men? In fact they were once more like angels than men. They have descended from the race of men and are, as you see them now, because they became so materialistic in their search for metals and gem stones that they took on the baser qualities of life such as 'greed'. However, they are on the upward life spiral again and are once again finding their synchronisation with nature while man is going in a downward spiral."

"Why do we have these wars?" asked Pazamor.

"Sometimes war is a necessary part in breaking down static structures and civilisations that have become stagnant. It is also a way for nature to keep control on the human population. However, if people would learn to share more; that is, give instead of take, and learn from each other, then wars would not be necessary as a controlling mechanism."

"So is God or the universe responsible for these wars, deaths and disease?"

"No, of course not, ultimately the blame is with us. It is our negative thought forms that create the bad weather around our world today, just as it is the positive forms that can restore it. It is man's fears, suspicions and greed that create the wars in our world today.

I heard a story that a disciple walked through a jungle of lions with no fear in his heart and they backed away from him. Such animals can smell fear and will always attack the weakest animal because of this – if they cannot detect it they will not attack.

You have read the ancient book called the Bible? In it there is the story of David and Goliath. While Goliath was a giant of a man David was but a small boy. However, David had no fear – in fact quite the opposite he believed and knew that he would defeat the giant – he took on the mantle of power and achieved his goal.

This is one reason that 500 people can defeat 2,000. If you are to succeed in your mission Paz, have no fear in your mind or heart."

*

While Pazamor and Tang were speaking, Duke had found the source of the smoke. It was indeed a party of about 200 but they were not trolls they were men! He looked around more carefully while remaining very still. They had indeed been building siege engines, Duke presumed they were to attack the monastery, but were still unfinished. Centre to them was a strange tent like none he had seen before – it was tall, round and decorated in gold and black. The soldiers were seated or standing around the camp with eyes fully open but they were not moving.

Something was very wrong! Duke continued to observe the soldiers themselves. They wore armour not too unlike his, though a little heaver and better protected. They also had long swords while he only ever used a short sword, dagger or a specially designed crossbow he had made himself. But most worrying of all they had the mark of the Nomad regiment. They were soldiers from Fort Nomad!

Duke was confused, why would soldiers from Fort Nomad seek to attack the monastery? It did not make any sense at all, though he was sure this tent had something to do with it.

He back-tracked to find Pazamor and Benedict talking. As he appeared Pazamor looked up and out of the corner of his eye noticed a shimmer of air surrounding Brother Benedict – Tang was gone again.

"Hi Duke," whispered Benedict, "What is the situation?"

"We have three choices the way I see it. We can skirt around them quietly and avoid them, go back to the monastery and help defend it, or we can attack!"

They both looked at Duke.

"What did you say? - Attack 200 trolls?" said Pazamor.

Duke laughed, "They are only humans not trolls."

Pazamor and Benedict smiled. So that is ok then?" asked Benedict.

"Look!" said Duke, "I know it sounds crazy but I believe I have a plan. It will need your help though. Brother do you have any anointing oil on you?"

"Yes, of course I do Duke – it's for healing."

"Can I borrow some?"

"Here," said Brother Benedict taking a small jar of oily looking liquid from one of his many pockets.

Duke took what looked like a miniature crossbow from behind his back that had been hidden under his cape.

"Paz, do you have any of that bread from your provisions handy?"

Pazamor grabbed his sack and found some of the bread in question and passed it to Duke.

"Help me Paz and make some of these." He rolled the bread around in a circle with his hands using a little oil and brought it back to a ball of dough that was saturated in oil.

Taking this he placed it through the head of the crossbow bolt and also rubbed oil over the wooden shaft.

"Can you make me five more of these Pazamor?" asked Duke.

Pazamor set to work.

"Benedict can you make a very small fire avoiding too much smoke?"

"No Duke you would be better at that. Give me your bolts and I will help Pazamor. You create the fire."

Duke produced about five smaller crossbow bolts from a holder around his belt and handed them to Pazamor and Benedict and they set to work.

"I have a candle Duke," said Benedict.

"Excellent! We should be able to do this quickly by working together, but we must hurry before the sun rises."

After Duke had created the fire Benedict lit his candle and quickly put out the fire. Pazamor and Duke then proceeded in the direction of the camped army while Benedict led the three horses further around the rear so that any noise created would be less obvious and hopefully unheard, and they could make a fast exit, if needed.

Both Pazamor and Duke surveyed the scene before them. It was unchanged from when Duke had left.

Duke was after the siege engines – they had been built to a monstrous size already but still unfinished if they were to scale the heights of the Celthina Monastery. He had reasoned that if they could destroy these wooden battle engines then they would give the monastery a few sunrises grace.

There were five of these giant boxes with ladders more than half constructed and being built in two parts.

Pazamor took the candle he had been carefully guarding from being extinguished and lighted the first bolt as Duke placed it in front of him and prepared the next ready to go.

Duke took his self-designed crossbow and wound the small winch to pull the bow's string only halfway back. He quickly aimed at the farthest siege engine he could see and fired before the crossbow itself could catch on fire. It whistled high in the air and struck its wooden target at the highest point.

Pazamor passed Duke the next bolt and lighted it, the burning oil dripping when fixed to the crossbow. They worked quickly firing the lighted bolts at their targets. Duke used some water a couple of times to put out any flames on his crossbow. The soldiers remained motionless like zombies, despite the whistling noise being created from the missiles.

Then they saw the tent move – a large flap opened and a tall person, dressed in a long black cloak emerged.

As Duke fired the fourth fire missile, the being that had emerged from the tent looked directly towards them. Duke still had one tower to hit, but was distracted by the cloaked being that was staring at him, and hit a tree instead.

By this time the first target was well alight and the soldiers were still entranced like lifeless statues – that was it - they were zombies! Transformed by the dark arts.

This black being before them must be controlled by a black wizard. Pazamor's eyes met with those of the black cloaked being – its eyes were also as black as coal.

"It's a 'shade'," said Duke. "Run Pazamor, run!"

Pazamor clumsily dropped the candle that had been in his hand. It landed on the floor and the bush they had been hiding behind went up in flames.

As they ran as fast as they could, they heard the wizard's shade speaking towards the zombies in its control, as if to direct them towards Pazamor and Duke.

However, the zombies did not like the fire in front of Pazamor or Duke and backed off from it in fear. The shade was undaunted by the fire or of them and continued towards them flying through bushes and screeching in anger.

Pazamor and Duke continued to run as fast as they could in what they thought must be the direction Benedict had taken.

The shade was closing in on them, when they suddenly saw Benedict up ahead.

"Have some Holy Water shade!" shouted Benedict as he threw a vial of water towards the shade.

The shade stopped in its tracks as the bottle hurtled towards it.

"Smash the bottle Duke!" he shouted.

Duke understood what Benedict was saying and as the bottle passed, flying towards the shade, he drew his short sword and broke the bottle in half with one clean sweep. The broken bottle continued to spin in the air towards the shade but with the water now released.

As the water touched the shade, it screamed in terror and the black being fell to the ground with some gas-like substance coming forth as if it had been evaporated on contact. The sun rose at the same point of contact and the bell of the monastery could be heard in the distance.

The soldiers fell to the floor and then got up – they had been released from the enchantment spell.

They quickly moved away from the fire that had been started and then when they realised what was happening began to put it out by clearing some of the trees in its way with axes they had been carrying and hitting the fire with their capes in an attempt to extinguish it.

The Sergeant of the Guard approached Pazamor, Duke and Benedict. He was looking tired but his eyes were now normal. Dressed in full battle armour he rattled as he moved.

"My men and I owe you our thanks, which of you is the leader?"

Pazamor, Duke and Benedict looked at each other as if to ask each other the same question. While none would have disagreed with Duke leading them, they saw each other as equals.

Pazamor tried to reply as such.

"You may address us all in that way," he said.

"Very well," said the Sergeant, addressing them all.

"About three sunrises ago the King came to our Fort with a few of his advance guard. He also had with him a Lord, by the name of Kraytos, I believe.

His guards' eyes were as black as the depths of hell and they seemed strangely immobile. The king sat next to the Lord and said he was here to inspect the safety of the 'great sword'.

I explained to him that it was still safe and well protected in our fort.

Nevertheless, he still wanted to see it.

I reminded him again that it was not possible to see the sword, as many summers ago on his command it had been protected by the Wizard Torrum and only such a white wizard could safely retrieve it. It was protected by many traps within the fort, including the Black Guard.

The Lord grew very agitated, stood up and spoke in a strange tongue while flapping his hands around at me and my men and that is all I remember before finding myself here in front of you."

"The sword's blade may still be safe within Fort Nomad. We should continue that way," said Pazamor.

The three of them agreed and after sitting with the Sergeant and sharing breakfast they continued on their way. The Sergeant and his troops headed towards the monastery for food supplies and Pazamor, Duke and Benedict towards Fort Nomad.

Chapter 6
Fort Nomad

As they left the edge of the forest and entered the desert plains the horses settled into a rhythmic stride and Pazamor admired the beauty of the desert scenery all around him, while Benedict and Duke talked of other interesting things. They travelled until the sun was at its highest point in the sky.

"Ouch!" said Pazamor as his horse stopped sharply and he was thrown forward a little.

"Let's take a break here," said Duke to Pazamor and Benedict.

Pazamor tried to dismount.

"Duke – could you help me please?" he had still not got the hang of getting off a horse by himself.

They tied the horses to a lone bush and all sat down to eat. Pazamor's backside and legs ached and he was glad to sit on ground that did not seem to be moving up and down.

While they ate, Pazamor tried to see Fort Nomad in the distance but instead saw the etheric currents or heat shimmering above the sands.

"How far is it Duke? Have you been there before?"

"We are about half-way there Paz and yes I have been there twice before."

"I too have been to Fort Nomad taking services in St John's Chapel, within the bailey," said Benedict.

"We need to conserve our energy Paz," said Duke in an unusually concerned tone, "It's best if we avoid talking too much until we get there."

Benedict nodded in agreement.

Pazamor shrugged his shoulders, as if to say 'whatever' and took out his small book from his cape and began reading:

'Words must be spoken with great care. They contain power within them, some more than others. The more ancient a word the more powerful it will tend to be. Some notes or sounds are also more powerful than others. Words can attract additional power and force if used in group form. Bad words like swear words can attract bad energies and forces to them and the forms they create, if created with the baser instincts, like anger or jealously, will often give them sharp defining edges and a dark red or muddy green colour with red particles within this. Beware the creator also, because at some point these thought forms will surely come back like a boomerang with either reduced or increased force to that sent.

If you send out thoughts of peace or protection in the form of a blessing then you can literally create small angels or symbols of power. If you direct it to a person or people then they can protect those you send them to. However, like any good builder you must construct these with care and spend time doing so – do not think too much of the person you send it to. Instead let the powers of the Universal Spirit work through you as a channel for love and peace and ask for their guidance in directing this energy to where it is needed most.

Indefinite forms are cloudlike in shape and float around as such, usually around the creator, either enhancing or reducing the aura they surround.

'A man sitting in his room and thinking right thoughts will be heard a hundred miles away.'

To the unskilled occultist the power of prayer is an easer form to start with, especially if you are passing on the thought form or words of power for a higher being to pass on for you, to wherever it is most needed.

With all thought forms it is great responsibility. If you have the eye of seeing then this is real – even if you do not you may train yourself to feel or see such vibrations as love or anger within your own aura and therefore recognise them in others.

Body language is worth a course of study.

You do not need to see the definite, muddy red, cone shaped arrows that will fly from someone that is shouting abuse towards you or another. What may seem as a magical world of colour and shape has its roots from the thoughts of beings all around – this is the world of the 'Deva'. DO NOT retaliate with the same course of action, rather send thoughts of love and blessing that will protect you and the one sent to.

The universal rule is:

'Keep the hearth of your thoughts pure'.

They reached Fort Nomad before the sun had set in the sky. Before them was a large motte and bailey type castle with the surrounding wooden or palisade walls painted white.

Pazamor stared in awe. There was visible damage to the inner bailey, most of the thatched roofs of the enclosed buildings had been badly damaged by fire, but some men were engaged in repairing them.   The higher motte was undamaged.

"Who goes there?" shouted a gruff voice from the first gate-tower at the entrance to the lower part of the castle, namely the bailey.

"Squire Duke is at your door. Open up!" shouted Duke, in a voice with great authority.

He held his cloak back to reveal a coat of arms on his chest which hung over his chain-mail.

The guard recognised this and wasted no time in quickly lowering a long wooden bridge across the large deep, trench surrounding the bailey. The trench was full of wooden spikes as further defence, as there was a lack of water available in these parts.

The Sergeant greeted them as they entered the bailey.

"Good evening," he said, welcoming them with a salute from his hand.

"Good evening," they all replied.

"What business do you have with Fort Nomad?" asked the Sergeant.

"We met your Sergeant and broke the enchantment spell held over him and his army. We are here as friends," said Brother Benedict.

The sergeant eyed Duke up and down and then held out his hand to Duke and the others in thanks.

"Then in friendship I welcome you to Fort Nomad. You may put your horses in our stables and have a meal in the Great Hall if you are quick. However, you will have to sleep in the Great Hall or the soldiers' quarters as the guests' quarters are still greatly damaged by the enchanted soldiers you met earlier.

Lord Kraytos was not able to enchant us all, and those, like myself, that were not drawn in by his evil magic ran to the upper hill of the motte and pulled up the drawbridge to protect ourselves. As he was not able to enter this section of our castle, he decided to set fire to what he could and took his new army towards the Celthina Monastery. I guess he would have made some siege engines to bring back and attack us further: at least that would have been my strategy."

"Why not use his magic to attack you?" asked Pazamor.

"I don't know much Sir, only that he was trying to steal what we are sworn to protect. He was not interested in killing us particularly, though I am sure if he felt he could gain by it he would not hesitate to do so."

"Thank you for the information Sergeant," said Duke, as they all left for the Great Hall after taking their horses to the stable.

As the three of them walked into the Great Hall their feet moved over rushes that were strewn over the floor. They sat around a warm open fire, surrounded by stone blocks in the middle of the hall. Some serving staff were starting to prepare for a night's sleep. While another served them. "What can I get ye good Sirs?" asked a small lady with a happy smile.

"What do you have?" asked Pazamor inquisitively.

Spotting the Brother amongst them she said, "Potato soup for 3 danks each or dove pie for four. What will it be?"

"The soup for me," said Pazamor.

"Me to," said Benedict.

"and I also," said Duke.

Then they all looked at each other as if to ask who will pay? The servant stood waiting as if thinking the same.

Father Benedict produced a ten dank piece – "Here you go," he said, "and keep the change my good lady." The servant girl took it and bowed in thanks.

Both Pazamor and Duke thanked Benedict as they realised that neither of them had much money on them for this journey and began to eat their warm evening meal, as the sun set in the evening sky.

A rat scurried by in the corner of the room, chased by a small dog that pounded on it and began to hungrily devour it.

Benedict spoke first.

"I think that Lord Kraytos cannot enter the motte, not because of the drawbridge but because it is protected by the white magic of Torrum. Kraytos being a dark wizard cannot enter – unless he had the help of the Enchanted Guards. If it had not been for the quick thinking sergeant we met earlier, then he may well have succeeded."

After a filling meal, Brother Benedict knelt down to pray. Duke lay on his back to sleep and Pazamor left to take some fresh air.

Outside the Great Hall he could feel the cool, fresh evening. The sun had been replaced by a near full-moon and stars. How bright and beautiful they were. Pazamor found a ladder leading up to the walkway that surrounded the bailey which gave a good vantage point. He climbed this and sat in a corner cross legged, with his back to the wooden palisade staring at the multitude of flickering radiant stars in the clear night sky.

As he sat he could see a meteor fly pass – 'wow!' he thought, as he admired the universe's beauty.

He closed his eyes and began to meditate. After thinking the Great Invocation he concentrated on his ajna chakra.

Within an instant he could feel a cool breeze behind the surface of his forehead and hear the low buzz of energy all around him. A while later he felt as if a cold metal band had been placed around the top of his head and he felt at total peace. A short time later he awoke from this state and returned to the Great Hall to sleep.

He had no difficulty finding the spot where his straw bedding had been placed; near the low glowing fire between the sleeping Duke and Benedict.

Pazamor settled down and thanked the Universal Spirit for looking after him and his friends and then dropped off to sleep.

As he came to a conscious awakening within his dreams he again found himself at the base of the mountain in the desert-like landscape. Alone he floated up to the cave entrance and entered the tunnel walking through its winding passage.

He knew where to travel, the only place he was permitted. When he reached the chanting room it was empty but the wall cloth had been moved back and the door left ajar. Pazamor continued through this and along another winding corridor drawn towards a small opening to find Benedict waiting.

"Greetings Young Paz, enter…" announced Benedict.

Benedict, Pazamor, Duke and Sapphira were seated in the chamber at a round table. At the head seat, which was more elaborately decorated than the rest, sat Benedict.

"Welcome Brothers and Sisters," said Benedict, looking towards Sapphira.

"As you may already know, the blade of the Sorcerer's Sword is kept on the motte part of Fort Nomad and is well protected by white magic. Only a magician like Sapphira or someone pure in heart like Pazamor could succeed in the task of retrieving it safely."

"Me?" asked Pazamor in surprise.

"Yes," said Benedict, "and Sapphira is too far away from our group, we need someone in the physical for this task and that person is you!"

"What must I do?" asked Pazamor with interest.

Sapphira replied, "You need to enter the motte and descend to the furthest point, whereupon you will find a protected trap door. You must find how to open this and enter.

Somewhere along the corridor, behind one of the closed doors, you will find the sword blade you seek, pick the wrong door and you will find death."

"And where is Kraytos now and what is he doing?" asked Pazamor.

"He left a shade in command of the army he had enchanted after failing to get the magic blade and then headed in the direction of Troll Tower. It is said that is where the magic gem is held and Torrum has given the task of protecting it to the Wood Trolls," said Sapphira.

"We must continue our training Pazamor," said Duke.

They all left the chamber together, the way they came and soon came upon the large wooden door with no handle or lock.

"Believe that you may enter and you will Pazamor," announced Sapphira, as she and Duke walked directly through it.

Pazamor found himself on his own again but could hear Benedict and other monks sounding the OM in the distance.

He looked at the door, calmed himself as if in meditation and simply walked through the door!

As he passed through it he felt very weird, as if his body broke into millions of smaller pieces and these tiny particles vibrating at a faster rate enabled him to pass through the space of the larger, slower vibrating particles of the door, merging together again on the other side.

Before him, what looked like a busy chemistry class greeted him. The students greeted Pazamor with applause as he entered the room. A tall figure cloaked in purple, stood at the front and beckoned Pazamor towards an empty desk, with various potions bubbling away.

Pazamor looked around and instinctively knew what to do: 'transmutation'. He was trying to recreate this effect. They all were.

He played with the potions before him with extreme enjoyment – you could say he was in his element!

The next day came by announcement from the call of a rude cockerel. The population of the bailey began to stir.

Benedict was the first of the party to awaken, followed by Pazamor and Duke. Pazamor could hear the chapel bell of the bailey signalling Morning Prayer and prepared himself to attend. Lots of singing took place in another tongue within and Pazamor, Benedict and Duke joined in as best they could.   Pazamor struggled with the chanting, but nevertheless enjoyed it greatly.

When they returned from the chapel to the Great Hall, the tables were re-assembled for breakfast. The morning meal consisted of bread and ale, which were made in the brew house, next to the Great Hall.

The same lady that served them the day before appeared and requested three danks each and looked to Brother Benedict for payment.   Brother Benedict smiled, "How about eight danks? I do not drink ale my good lady."

"Of course Brother," she said, "will hot water be fine?"

"Yes – thank you – may the Universal Spirit bless you."

Many soldiers were present for breakfast and they did not have to pay, as food and lodging was a part of their wage.

When all were seated the Chaplin, who had lead the prayers in the church, rose to bless the food and drink for all present.

Pazamor closed his eyes to listen carefully to the Chaplin, with his hands interlocked in a sign of prayer.

"As we begin this new day before us, let us remember the night before. It was dark, empty and quiet not unlike death, yet this beautiful morning is bright and full of bustling life. Light and darkness are two sides of the same coin, a coin which we are always throwing randomly in the air of life and hoping it lands on the side of good.

Yes, it is best to look at this good side and remain positive with all things in life even when the coin lands on the dark side.

Find the good in all things my friends and you will find eternal happiness.

Enjoy your lovely food and thank you Universal Spirit for your love all around us for even when the sun is hidden by the clouds – it is but for a short time and you are always with us, in this life and the next."

Everyone uttered, "OM... OM ... OM..." rising to a crescendo until eventually fading away into silence ...

They waited for a very short time in the peace of silence and then returned to eat and drink.

"Can you remember the dream last night Pazamor?" asked Duke.

"Ummn – no," replied Pazamor, "you?"

Duke and Benedict laughed.

"Your ignorance may some day save your life Young Paz," laughed Brother Benedict.

"What did I do?" asked Pazamor confused.

"Oh Paz," laughed Duke "You got a good night's sleep it seems!" laughed Duke even more loudly.

"Oh come on guys – what happened – I can't remember!" said Pazamor.

Benedict continued, "You have volunteered to take on a difficult task for all of us. You will use your skill to open a trap door at the bottom of the motte, make your way down a passage with many doors, select the one behind which the Sorcerer's Sword blade resides. You must pick the right one for the other doors open up to deadly traps. Only a white wizard or one of pure heart may enter the trap door mentioned – you are our choice Pazamor."

Pazamor listened intently and remembered his time with the Cave Troll. He had passed that test. Why not this one?

"Ok," said Pazamor, "I accept the challenge. Let's go!"

"I will speak to the Sergeant first," said Duke, "I know him and he knows my father." Duke left and spoke to a man at arms to find the location of the Sergeant. After a while he returned.

"You have permission to enter the motte and retrieve the sword blade Paz. The Sergeant will escort you personally."

Pazamor hugged Benedict and Duke and vowed to return soon with the sword's blade.

The Sergeant of the Guard greeted Pazamor and led him towards a large wooden bridge that extended to the motte. A drawbridge was lowered, connecting this, and they entered the surrounding enclosure housing the tall keep. The Sergeant led Pazamor to the east side of the keep and up a ladder to an opening on the first floor.

Once inside the Sergeant unlocked a door leading to a wooden staircase.

The Sergeant shook Pazamor's hand and bid him good luck before Pazamor descended below.

Chapter 7
The Sorcerer's Sword

Pazamor was descending the creaky wooden stairway of the cellar when he noticed the second to last step was different from the rest and was a little loose. While standing on the floor at the bottom he closely examined the step only to find he could carefully remove the top and side of it to reveal another hidden step within, but made of glass! From the bottom of the stairway he could dimly see a large golden metal trap door with mysterious symbols covering it.

He gently touched this. Passing his hand over it, he noticed that it felt strange, as if full of energy. In the middle of the door was a simple large iron ring that looked as if a rope may have once been through it – perhaps it had been used to lift this large door into place?

The door was set into a solid cobbled floor of tightly packed small stones. Pazamor was not entirely sure what to do – he sat down to meditate and think of a way to open the trap door.

As he sat and concentrated he thought about what direction to take – 'direction!' he thought.

He awoke from the meditation quickly and looked again at the symbols covering the trap door, by now his eyes had acclimatised to the low light and he could see all around much better. Yes, there in the middle, surrounding the ring, was a symbolic compass.

He rummaged through his pockets to produce his father's compass and looked carefully at the two, comparing them.

His compass lined up with that of the one on the floor. North pointed to the way he had come, to the staircase and up. He looked to the east, it had a white symbol for earth. He laughed to himself, as he knew the churches were always aligned this way with the alter in the east. The south point had the symbol of water and was coloured blue. The west point had the symbol for air and gases and was coloured red.

Looking again at the compass point it reminded him of a star and the north point had the symbol of a golden full moon surrounding by fire.

Pazamor rushed up the staircase to the room above and then another set of stairs to the highest point he could find where he reached another trap door above his head, one that was silver and also had the sign of the compass and similar intricate patterns to that of the one below. However, when he compared his compass with this one below it was aligned the reverse way around. Where his compass pointed north, this wooden engraving pointed south – again towards the stairs he had just ascended.

Pazamor called to the Sergeant to assist him. The Sergeant arrived and produced a key that unlocked the top trap door and Pazamor lifted it straight up with the help of the Sergeant, carefully observing the way it opened.

The door had a white crystal in the position where the moon was situated on the one below. He also noticed this wooden trap door was not a perfect square unlike the one below. Pazamor smiled, he turned the door a half-turn and placed it down again. He looked at the white crystal and could see the light of the sun penetrating it and entering below.

He gave the key back to the Sergeant and again went down to the cellar of the keep. Looking up from the staircase he could make out the crystal above in the wooden trap door – it glistened in the sun as it shone down deep into the cellar. Pazamor snuffed out the one and only torch light in the cellar and waited for his eyes to become accustomed to the darkness.

He sat at the back of the room in a meditative posture and carefully looked back towards the steps he had ascended.

Pazamor could see a small beam of light hitting the uneven glass step and noticed this light reflected as if the step was a prism. The light was bent directly to the metal trap door towards the central point but nothing happened.

Pazamor began to meditate again for the solution to this conundrum, he looked carefully at the symbols in the door on the floor and studied them in more detail.

He recognised the symbol of the trolls and one for sleep. He knew that these pictures and symbols gave a clue to what lay below and the possible answer to retrieving the blade.

A morning passed. Pazamor prayed to the Universal Spirit for help.

The Sergeant shouted down.

"Would you like a drink Sir? It gets pretty hot this time of the day."

"This time of day," thought Pazamor.

Maybe the door was designed to be opened at night under the light of the full moon – at least that is what he would try tonight.

Pazamor climbed the stairs to greet the Sergeant.

"Ok thank you Sergeant – I will have some food and ale if there is some available for free?"

"If you are a friend of Duke then this is not a problem Pazamor – do you mind if we talk a bit?"

The Sergeant waived and shouted down to a man at arms to bring food and ale. They both made their way to the topmost door of the tower, and into an open space overlooking the bailey and the land below.

While eating and drinking their midday meal they talked.

"Pazamor, I know little about you but understand your mission. You are attempting to retrieve the blade of the Sorcerer's Sword and that can only mean the other pieces of the sword also. That sword is very special. I remember seeing it in the Devian War when I was but a foot soldier. It's magical and has great power. It's said that whoever holds it will have control over the entire Troll kingdom.

At that time, when we were at war with the Trolls and they were winning, it enabled us to recover our positions and literally stop them in their tracks. The Wizard Torrum was the one that wielded it then, and from what I remember, he held it high in the sky at night and shouted some words of power and a mystical blue light surrounded us all. The Trolls ran away screaming, apart from one of their leaders, who was blind from the battle - a Wood Troll, from the Guild of Clerics.

We were about to descend on him to finish him off when the wizard lifted his hand and shouted, 'NO! There has been enough killing this day'.

One of the chief conjurers by the name of Kraytos suggested we had only just started and that we should finish the job and that he should have the sword and take on such a role if the Wizard Torrum was too old for the job.

Torrum realised that from that point on he would have to hide the sword and as he was in control of our regiment at the time, as our captain had been killed in battle, he took upon himself the task to break the sword into parts and spread it across the land. He gave me the sword's blade and the gemstone to the blind Troll. He took the sword's hilt himself and it is not sure where this part was stored or who he gave the task to.

We then all disbanded and went back to recreating our lives. It was known then that Kraytos had been changed by the war, changed for the worse and many of us had been badly affected. If Kraytos seeks the sword, then it will not be for good and if you are the one sent by Torrum, either directly or not directly, then I would rather help you than him."

Pazamor listened intently.

"I am no warrior or wizard," he said, "how will I be able to use such a sword?"

"You will find a way Pazamor."

Pazamor sat down to continue reading his book:

'Sound is associated with colour – if a note is sounded, colour can be seen corresponding to the note sounded, by one with the eye of seeing. Music itself can leave many coloured impressions that can emanate for a longer period than the notes heard. Certain musicians can emanate a signature similar to that in their own writing, so you can differentiate their own unique form of work through the colours formed from their music. For bigger energy signals, instruments like an organ are far superior to a piano. In the same way a band playing a particular note will create a greater energy signature than that of a person playing by themselves.

Peoples intelligence makes a difference to such forms – if added it greatly increases the power of the forms created and can give them more definition and lasting energy.'

Pazamor wondered about the sacred word OM and what type of colour it might produce? Just how much power for good could be generated from a church's steeple or Wizard's Tower as a transmitter of such energy for good?

As the night approached, Pazamor again entered the cellar of the Keep. He sat in the corner of the room in a meditative posture, concentrating on his ajna chakra but keeping his eyes open while watching the trap door in front of him with some trepidation.

He noticed a feint blue and white glow surrounding the edges of the trapdoor and wooden barrels nearby.

A small beam of white light fell from the crystal from the upper trapdoor above and as it hit the glass step below it was deflected through this and onto the golden metal trap door.

Pazamor sat patiently and watched the beam as it moved with time, it also got stronger and brighter with the light of the full moon. He carefully observed the movement to interpret where the beam would fall next and what it might release.

He examined the patterns on the door. He was looking for a crystal similar to the one above but saw nothing obvious.

The beam of light seemed to be moving around the door on the floor in a circular, clockwise direction. The prism inside the step must have been built to the highest standard. Much time passed and then he heard a click – the light had rotated full circle and was illuminating the north point.

Pazamor carefully approached the trap door, placed his hands through the metal ring in the centre of the door and pulled with all his might. He could feel it moving but only just – he would need the help of his friends.

Pazamor sat again in a meditative posture concentrated on his throat chakra briefly until he could feel it buzzing and then thought of the picture form he used for the word help. He sent this to Duke and concentrated on the form of Duke and his ajna chakra very briefly, then concentrating on the symbol again, he just waited.

Duke and Benedict eventually appeared.

"You called," smiled Duke.

"You got my message then Duke."

"It was a bit broken up into smaller shapes Paz but I knew it was you and rather than send a reply I thought it was quicker to come to you directly – so what's up?"

Pazamor smiled, "Can you help me lift the trapdoor?" he said.

Benedict looked closely at some of the symbols.

"You have released the lock Paz. That is excellent! However, the door is not meant to be lifted by hands but by sound."

"I will help you. We all need to sound this note." Benedict sounded a particular note from his throat that vibrated like a mix of notes Pazamor and Duke copied him and noticed the door start to rise before them. Benedict motioned for Paz and Duke to continue their chant and when the trap door had risen to the height of their shoulders Benedict changed the tone of his note and the door flew past them all, crashing into the wall.

Benedict laughed loudly – "Sorry, I have not tried this too many times before and obviously need more practice."

They all stared below.

"Well Paz, good luck! We will await your successful return," said Duke confidently.

Pazamor clasped wrists with both Benedict and Duke, shaking them before descending the winding steps into the darkness below.

He reached the bottom and while he could see the light above, it was difficult to make out anything while his eyes were still accustoming to the dim light of the cold cramped chamber he found himself in.

Eventually Pazamor could make out the shape of a long stone slab, similar to a tombstone, near the steps he had just climbed down. It was similar in size and shape to the one he had laid on in the Celthina Monastery. He began to ponder on what to do next, one side of him wanted to stay and think more, while the other wanted to rush onwards.

Before he knew any more, he was on his way down a corridor towards another door directly in front, using the dim green light from the lode stone around his neck to light his way. As he walked he passed many other doors on his left and right. Should he try one of these first? Something told him no – it was that small voice of intuition that we often override in life.

Pazamor tried the door and as he opened it he noticed his boot lace was undone, something made him bend down to tie it. At the same time the door opened fully and there was a phweesh! A large spear flew past his head and embedded itself in the wall behind him. It was a trap and if he hadn't bent down at that point in time he would have surely been killed.

Pazamor looked at all the doors before him, there were still eleven unopened and he felt sure that ten of these would contain deadly traps of some sort or another.

Pazamor returned to the room with the stone slab where he sat cross-legged on it to ponder further. Then he realised why he had been picked for the task. He would have to utilise his astral body to enter the doors without opening them in order to locate the sword's blade. That would be the easy bit! Would he remember the right door when he awoke?

Pazamor lay down and after falling asleep, he jumped from his body. He saw the physical shell left lying on the stone bed. Pazamor made his way along the corridor again - it glowed in a golden light. After walking through seven of the twelve doors he found the right one - it was the only one to have yet another door within it; but this door was made of lead and he could not penetrate it with his astral body.

He awoke from what felt like a dream and taking his lode stone to dimly light the way, walked down the corridor to what he felt was the seventh door – but was it?

He opened it slowly and quickly jumped aside – just in case it was the wrong one!

Nothing happened. He was in an open room that revealed the heavy lead door.

This door was covered in symbols. It had no obvious means of opening it and as he had not penetrated it when dreaming he was not sure what lay behind or indeed if it was yet another trap.

Pazamor found himself once again sitting in a meditative posture, carefully examining the door before him.

He immediately noticed a hole in the central part of the door; it was the size of the stone he had been given by the Wood Troll some sunrises before. He recognised similar symbols upon it. Carefully taking the stone in both hands he placed it in the hole in the middle of the door – it fitted perfectly and gave a soft green glow which grew brighter after being inserted. Pazamor could see the room quite clearly now. The brighter light created from the stone in the door illuminated the room displaying wooden panelling around the walls and an arched roof like a gigantic barrel.

He heard a clicking sound and the large lead door began to open inwards – within was darkness. The stone glowed less brightly again now that the door was open. Pazamor instinctively took the green stone from the door and held it in the air to light his way.   What lay before him did not feel man-made – an expanse of tunnels in all directions as if they had once been mines of some sort. Pazamor moved slowly ahead – he hadn't a clue on what to do next.

He took out his compass and looked to the east and reasoned that if he kept moving in one direction at least he would be able to get back. After travelling along the east tunnel for some time he saw the sword before him set in the wall.   He approached slowly – it was magnificent! Solid silver, razor sharp – the size of a double handed blade and beautifully crafted with symbols similar to those on the lode stone and doors within the cellar of the Keep.

As he took it off the wall he was sure some low pitched sound was created but thought little else of it until he could hear the thudding of heavy footsteps coming towards him – it was the sound of Cave Trolls from the north and south, who must have been given the task of guarding the sword.

Pazamor remembered the stone and once again held it in front of him as the trolls came into view. These were of a grey colouring but like the last one he had encountered they did not like the green light emanating from the stone one bit. Pazamor advanced with the gem in his hand, the trolls growling and flaying their hands around but unable to reach Pazamor, wincing back, as if in pain.

Clutching the heavy sword blade he quickly retraced his steps and eventually found his way safely back to his friends.

The whole company of Fort Nomad came forward to see who it was that had managed to retrieve the sorcerer's blade and stood in awe at the figure of Pazamor and his achievement.   The Sergeant saluted and stood with the Captain of the Guard who had managed to return safely to the fort with the rest of his regiment earlier that day.

"Well done Sir Pazamor," said the captain, "you have done what no man has ever done before you."

Everyone cheered and clapped as if a miracle had taken place that day.   Benedict and Duke approached and again tapped Pazamor on the shoulder.

"You did good friend, you did good!" said Duke.

Benedict smiled and blessed Pazamor.

"Peace to our world – love to all, not war!" shouted Pazamor at the top of his voice, holding forth the sword blade in the air high above his head. The blade shone in the light of the full moon and open fires around the camp.

Today had been a good day.

Chapter 8
Wizards' Way

The morning light broke over a misty etheric landscape. Trees were but small shadows from this great vantage point, mountain tops could be seen above these thick clouds of mist and it was as if they were floating on air.

Sapphira stared out of her tower window, wondering how Pazamor and Duke were performing in their part of the challenge. She looked at 'Randolph' her pet miner bird as he sat crowing contentedly, while she stroked the feathers on his head slowly in one direction.

Her room, while very small, contained everything she needed: a miniature library full of fascinating books of spells, healing, alchemy, demonology and other rare information. A cabinet packed with various crystals, herbs, exotic powders and other potions.

She had the luxury of a long wooden bed, chair, table and magic crystal lamp for reading her many books late into the night.

"Sapphira have you seen my magic eyes?" shouted Torrum, who was obviously awake by now.

'He's lost them again!' thought Sapphira.

She opened her door and proceeded to the top most part of the tower to where Torrum lived and worked.

'KNOCK! KNOCK! Sapphira beat at the door as hard as she could – the old wizard had a reputation for being so involved with his work that he often did not hear things around him.

"Come in, come in – don't wait around outside all day."

As she entered the large room a strange pungent smell greeted her nostrils.

Hunched over a bench was the great wizard Torrum, with a large open spell book and a multitude of different coloured liquids bubbling away.

"Hello Sapphira – have you seen my glasses? I am having problems reading this book."

Sapphira closed her eyes and pictured the magic eyes in her mind's eye and commanded – 'magic eyes show yourself!' She opened her eyes and felt drawn to the tallest book case in the room, sure enough they were there. Sapphira grabbed them from the top most shelves and drew the conclusion that Torrum must have left it there when bringing down the big spell book he had in his hand. She handed the crystal disks to Torrum.

"Thank you," he said in a relived tone. "No matter how many times I cast this spell I cannot seem to reverse the effect Sapphira."

"Oh, Torrum I am sure you will find the answer. You never give up – May the Light of the Universal Spirit guide you."

Torrum placed the crystal disks contained in a gold frame on his nose and put down what he was working on.

"Come here, my best student, come sit with me a while."

Sapphira sat facing Torrum after turning a stool to face him.

"You have told me that your group is obtaining the sword's blade from Fort Nomad and the great stone from Black Vintigan Forrest – but what of the sword's hilt? Sapphira, I must send you on this difficult and dangerous mission – if you would accept?"

"Of course Master,"

"Go on ahead of them, after first gaining provisions for the journey to Port Kepland and meet with a person called 'Jack the Rabbit' in the Black Swan's Tavern, he will be valuable for any information and may know were the sword's handle is kept."

"Very well Master, I will travel today," Sapphira spoke determinedly.

A shimmer in time and space came over Torrum:

"Remember white magic is black's opposite but in using it against this ensure you are using it in defence. Use the enemies own force against itself. If you should simply attack through anger, grief or of the other base astral emotions then you will invoke bad energy upon yourself. Be detached in your spell casting from that of the emotions. Use your higher self to achieve that which you would otherwise struggle with."

Torrum blinked and then said, "Are you still here Sapphira? I thought you were going?"

"Yes, of course Master, right away."

Torrum returned to his bench and his work of trying to reverse the 'Kraytos' spell.

Sapphira left the tower room and walked slowly down the long winding steps, eventually reaching the bottom and left by a large golden double door.

Wizard's Way was very busy by now. Market stalls had set up for the day and trading had already started.

Sapphira was wearing her favourite blue and purple cloak that shifted between two colours, depending on the intensity of the sunlight – purple for a bright day and dark blue for night – at the moment it was a bright purple. Around her waist hung a leather belt, a small dagger attached, but hidden from view, along with several small pouches containing money, stones and other useful items of assistance in magic.

Around her head of long, golden flowing hair she wore a gold band with a set blue jewel in the middle, conveniently placed over her forehead, in the position of her ajna chakra.

Not a person to travel alone, she had decided to create a familiar to escort her. She found one of the many quite small temple buildings built for just one person and entered. Then she prepared a fire on the floor in front of her by simply taking from her belt two finger sized glass flasks of different coloured liquids from her belt and throwing them together, the fire being created as the two liquids met.

Sitting down before the fire in a meditative posture she took some ordinary dirt from the ground and threw it into the fire, while making several incantations.

Small sparks began to fly, spitting like a venomous snake.

She closed her eyes and in her mind's eye saw a Hoblin – a much smaller version of a Goblin. She opened her eyes and repeated the process twice before commanding the Hoblin to step forth from its world into ours.

Flash! Phweet! And a small earthen coloured Hoblin appeared before her. The fire was now completely gone, having served its purpose.

"What shall I call you Hoblin?" she said, quizzing herself.

"My name is Haddon, pretty lady," said the Hoblin.

"Very well then Haddon, will you accompany me on my mission and travels?"

"If it be for good and I get to make instead of destroy things then yes, but if you make me do bad things then I will expect to take a part of you…"

"Yes, I know the rules of sorcery Haddon," smiled Sapphira from the heart.

Haddon was an interesting type of Deva. Many ordinary folk would not be able to see him at all, though some few may see him as a small ball of bright energy.

Normally he worked with nature – he ensured trees got their water and kept disease away from some of the more advanced plants within that kingdom. However, today he was accompanying Sapphira, a white wizard, someone who could see, hear and understand him.

Sapphira jumped up with Haddon in tow.

She knew she needed to replace some of the potions she had just used in the creation of Haddon and also stock up on more micro-flasks to hold them in.

Sapphira moved very much like a ghost, her feet hidden by her long robes, she seemed to glide along as if floating on air.

After replenishing her potions and micro flasks from a store for her leather belt with some money and trading of services (She cured some warts from a child for four danks – though it was the child's fault for playing with its father's potions without permission).

She started on her long journey with Haddon in tow. Who very nicely materialised some strawberries, seemingly from thin air. He wasn't quick enough for Sapphira though.

"I saw the seeds," she said, toying with him.

"Oh drat," said Haddon smiling – you wizards don't miss a trick!"

Sapphira could have done the same by speeding up nature to create real strawberries from just seeds. Though many would have called this a miracle, to the Masters, Wizards, Devas and some of the clerics it was just a natural thing.

They shared the juicy strawberries together while walking along a worn dusty forest path.

As Sapphira crunched her teeth into the juicy fruits she could feel the extra rush of energy – Haddon had created them with love and added even more energetic value to them by sharing them in this way.

They soon came to a large deep fast flowing river that blocked their path with no bridge in view in either direction. Sapphira and Haddon mused.

"Ok," said Sapphira, "I can do this – I just need to generate the right kind of energy field."

She sat in a meditative posture and in her mind's eye saw herself crossing the river by simply walking across it and being on the other side.

After a while she came out of her meditation with the energy field she required surrounding her, she knew it was there as she could hear the light buzzing sound of energy in her spiritual ears.

They both stood in front of the fast flowing river then without warning Sapphira simply walked across it, as if floating on air. She could feel the cold water under her feet as she crossed but did not sink. Haddon looked on and clapped in appreciation, then he leapt across the river in three giant leaps, like a flat stone flipped across the waters surface.

It was Sapphira's time to clap now.

"Well done," she said in admiration, smiling softly at Haddon.

Haddon pointed to Sapphira's cloak which was wet on the bottom. She laughed to herself knowing what Haddon meant by the joke – if she had been a Master her cloak would still be dry!

Haddon certainly had a sense of humour, something much needed in life. She could imagine Haddon running circles around the non-initiated and confusing them or losing them in the forests of Dronagon just for fun. Most nature spirits took to such play.

Both Sapphira and Haddon enjoyed the beautiful scenery of nature before them.

Sapphira breathed in the fresh air around them. Each tree brought its own unique smell and shape. Sapphira moved through the forest softly and silently. In the air above she could see what looked like a miner bird, flying high above them and travelling towards Wizard's Way.

The sky itself was clear, except for a few high clouds. The sun's morning rays were warm on Sapphira's face. She smiled with happiness, as she travelled through this peaceful place with Haddon running behind.

On the forest floor small wood ants scurried by, picking up what they could use for nesting material.

Sapphira noticed a particular type of yellow mushroom she knew to be safe and talked to the plant quietly. She explained that she needed some of its energy and thanked the plant for its gift of food. Carefully picking three of the mushrooms and leaving two behind she placed them in a small pouch around her belt for later and continued to forage as they moved onward. She had learnt the art of foraging from Duke some summers ago and taught Duke the art of telepathy in return.

Haddon watched Sapphira intently.

"It is good that you treat nature with such love – in its turn nature will treat you."

Sapphira found nuts on the forest floor and gathered in another pouch. When the sun was at its highest point in the sky they stopped. Sapphira needed to eat to give her physical body energy. She produced water from a small metal flask and poured some of this into the lid, in which she prepared to cook the mushrooms and nuts.

She got some small twigs together and made a tripod to hold the flask and made some room underneath ready to create her magical fire.

"I will do that for you - save your special flasks," said Haddon as he spun around fast, turning into a ball of light and moving directly under the flask produced some dry moss and more twigs, then heating himself to the required temperature he ignited the dry moss, which in turn lit the twigs and created the fire needed to heat the water and boil the mushrooms and nuts making a very refreshing nutritious meal.

"I could have just heated the water by raising my body heat Sapphira but that would have taken more energy than the method thus employed."

Sapphira smiled, "Yes, I understand that Haddon. My Master Torrum has reduced water to ice by lowering his own body temperature and extending it to that which he wished to freeze, but I am still learning that one."

"Why don't you try now?"

"I could try at the next meal?"

"Ok."

Sapphira sat down to meditate and Haddon fed off some of the energy like someone warming their hands around a hot fire. Like all Devas in this world, he did not need food in the physical sense but still needed energy. As a Deva he could collect this energy through the sun or from other spiritual beings. Normally he and Devas like him would grab such energy from unsuspecting humans, by simply touching them in the crowds of cities. They would not grab too much energy, just enough to make them strong and the humans a little tired.

Sapphira understood this and while she was able to draw her own energy directly from the Universal Spirit she did not mind Haddon taking some of this energy for himself – indeed she offered it to him as a friend.

While she meditated on her ajna chakra she could feel her eyes roll up towards her forehead and hear the buzz of energy surrounding her as she was absorbed into the bright white light before her. She stood silently in her mind while concentrating and at total peace.

Sometime later she awoke. The fire was out and Haddon had disappeared.

She thought this strange and looked around the makeshift camp but could find no clues as to what might have happened to Haddon.

Her intuition that told her that danger was nearby but not what it might be. She quickly assessed the area around her for possible attacks, but nothing obvious stood out. Then a bolt from a crossbow flew through the air narrowly missing her as she turned her body to the side.

She worked out the direction but now another three such bolts hurtled towards her. Bandits!

She imagined in her mind's eye a wall of stone and held up her robe in front of her, energising it with the power from the meditation she had just performed. The bolts hit the robe and it was as if time and space stood still. She could see one of the arrows was meant for her heart, but instead it hit the robe and simply fell to the ground, without even putting a hole in it. Though a pressure mark on the robe was visible, it had not been torn by the crossbow's bolt.

Then she heard them running towards her, six highly armoured guards, long swords flying around them as they charged.

"STOP!" she commanded with no fear in her voice; aimed directly at them with such spiritual force that they were knocked over as if they had just run into a solid wall.

Four of them were out cold, the other two slowly got up rubbing their sore heads and staring as if they did not know where they were.

"What happened?" said one of them.

Sapphira was about to let down her guard when she felt an evil energy nearby. It was not emanating from the guards but from a dark shape that came flying towards her.

The guards moved out of the way quickly. She recognised the dark shape as a shade. She tried to cast a counter spell but the shade was on her before she could utter the spell. The soldiers that could stand ran back to the forest from which they came, freed from the enchantment spell that must have been under the shade's command.

As the shade touched her she felt her energy drain and she fell to the ground weak but still conscious – 'God help me!' she thought, as she felt her energy and life force being sucked away by this malevolent being floating over her as she lay defenceless on the floor.

She was about to lose consciousness when she saw the brightest white light she had ever seen engulf herself and everything around her. She began to wonder if she had actually died.

Then she heard a familiar voice, "Can I give you a hand?"

It was the Wizard Torrum with Haddon floating near his shoulder.

Haddon looked concerned.

"Your friend appeared to me in my study very worried, he explained that he noticed the shade from a distance and that it saw your light and was attracted to it the same way any Deva would be. He also told me of a small army it commanded and that it was on its way to Wizards' Way. I had to come quickly. Needless to say Sapphira I logged into your energy signature and Haddon guided me here in a flash of light - I do not think these shades like the light too much!" he said, pointing to the scorched grass beside them, which was the only visible remains of the shade which had fallen after leaving the safety of the dark forest to attack Sapphira.

"Well, I must get back to my work and you must continue on your journey Sapphira. Get some rest first and take care, my able student."

Chapter 9
Black Vintigan Forest

After a day's travel through the rough desert of Nomad's Land, facing freak sandstorms and negotiating large sand dunes, Pazamor, Duke and Benedict reached the edge of the fabled Black Vintigan Forest. They dismounted and while Pazamor and Benedict rested the horses and themselves, Duke searched for a good place to camp.

Duke crossed his eyes, blurring his normal vision, and carefully looked around the surrounding area for any power spots capable of giving them energy rather than taking it. One spot near a broken tree was dark in colour and its energy felt draining, even from this distance. On more careful inspection, Duke could see the remains of a dead animal beneath it; this was a bad spot!

He climbed a small hill and continued his search more carefully, while looking for the right type of aura; he also used his intuition to guide him. One spot looked perfect: a large flat granite rock that stuck out of the ground by an arm's length. This would do.

"Hey, Paz, Ben, I have found a good place to camp. Let's go!"

"Yes, Sir!" said Pazamor standing to attention in a joking manner.

They all gathered around the large rock Duke had discovered and agreed it was a good place to rest. Duke secured the horses, while Benedict found some wood and rocks to make a campfire. It was Pazamor's turn to find some food. He carefully surveyed the area around them and in particular noticed the variety of trees. One stood out in particular, the tree seemed to have some fruit suspended from it and as he approached closer his suspicions were confirmed. As he stood in front of the tree he smiled - it was full of apples.

He wondered how to get the delicious looking fruit down from the tree. It was too big to shake and didn't look very climbable. He reasoned that he could throw a stick and try his luck at knocking the apples off one by one, but that if he had a rope he stood a better chance of lassoing the branch and tugging it down towards him, so that he could reach the fruit more easily. Unfortunately, the only problem with that idea was that he did not have such a rope ... or did he?

Pazamor rushed up the hill again back towards the camp. The sun's rays were low in the sky now and Benedict had finished gathering wood and was busy building the fire.

"Can I borrow your belt please?" asked Pazamor, pointing at Benedict's robe.

Benedict looked puzzled and then realised what Pazamor meant. "You mean my rope belt?" he said.

"Yes, that's right. I only need it for a short time."

"Ok, look after it then please," said Benedict handing over the rope that tied his waist and held his robe in.

Pazamor returned with the rope and eight apples.

"Thanks Paz I will make a soup from this. Can you find some more of this herb?" said Benedict holding up a small leaf, from a small wooden box with many compartments, which he then passed to Pazamor.

"Yes, sure," said Pazamor, taking the leaf and leaving once again.

Pazamor continued to search after placing a clear picture of the herb in his mind's eye and seeing himself finding it – his two hands grasping the discovery clearly.

He carefully lowered his bodies' vibration and moved more slowly and peacefully through the bushes around him, his image still tightly within his mind.

Then suddenly in front of him behind a bush appeared the herb he was looking for. He wasn't sure if he had found it through magnetism or if it had been created by a Deva for him – but whichever he thanked the Universal Spirit and grabbed most of the plant just leaving enough for the plant to continue its existence and hopefully in the essence of time create more of itself.

He was about to leave back for the camp when his spiritual ears heard the noise of running water in the distance. He carefully placed the herbs in his sack and went in the direction of the stream he could hear. He let his ears guide him and then he found it – a small bubbling brook, coming through the hill. He grabbed his water flask and drank all that he could then he carefully refilled it with the water he had found.

Pazamor took a stick and a red piece of cloth he had in his pocket. Tying the two together he made a marker for the stream and returned to the camp, picking some fresh dandelion leaves on the way.

Duke returned to the camp at about the same time.

"I found some water," announced Pazamor proudly.

"That's great Paz, we will fill up before we leave tomorrow."

"I will water the horses then," said Benedict. After getting instructions from Pazamor on the location of the water he gathered the horses and left to find the tranquil spot as described by Pazamor.

"I found some mushrooms Paz," said Duke.

They both sat around the campfire, which had not yet been lit. Duke took a small knife and carefully peeled the mushrooms before throwing them into the small cooking pot that had been provided by Benedict. He was probably the best cook of the three and when he returned with the horses and more water, their cans were once again full; he set to work on cooking their home-made soup.

Benedict effortlessly chopped all the ingredients they had gathered into fine pieces and threw them together into the pot, after having first boiled the water. He lifted the pot higher above the open fire onto another notch on the wooden branch overhanging the fire and this enabled the soup to simmer away instead of boil into nothing. After a while he threw a white substance into it and explained it was an important ingredient to give flavour.

The three of them huddled around the fire, while leaning against the large rock, which acted as a heater and a reasonable back rest for the three of them. They watched the sun, a pure disc of bright orange, setting in the sky, the horizon full of orange and purple hues as it descended towards the earth.

Birds in the air flocked to the forest trees to sleep for the night.

But despite enjoying all the amazing colours and sounds of nature all around him Pazamor missed the comfort of his bed and home cooked foods.

Benedict stirred the soup several more times – the apples having now turned to a mush and the other ingredients adding flavour.

Pazamor's tummy rumbled and even Duke looked on in expectation – it smelt wonderful – far better than if he or Duke had cooked it.

Benedict filled three cups and they all drank slowly of the soup he had made.

Wow! – What flavour! He certainly knew how to cook.

"So what is the secret?" asked Pazamor nudging Benedict's shoulder and making him tip a little of his soup.

"The secret of any good food is three fold Young Pazamor, spoke Benedict slowly and staring him directly in the eyes. "First you need good ingredients; two you need to cook the food to perfection – to the point you can smell the ingredients being released and merged together as one; third, and most important of all, you must put love into your food."

I always cook when I am happy and pray quietly in my mind while cooking. I will think things like 'I am adding love to this food' while stirring. It is important to eat slowly and likewise, if you wish to energise the food you eat – give thanks to the Universal Spirit and repeat positive statements like 'I am assimilating peace' or 'I am assimilating love' as you are eating the food or drinking the drink.

Duke threw some more wood onto the fire as the final strands of light disappeared, revealing a fantastic sunset full of warmth and love. It was as if the Universal Spirit was blessing them and the day. As the sun sank on the horizon the moon could be seen rising and the stars began to twinkle like bright diamonds set on a black marble surface.

Duke lay on the flat stone behind them covering himself with a blanket from his horse. Benedict knelt to pray and Pazamor realised it was time to sleep. However, he felt he could read a couple more pages of his book first and taking it from his cloak pocket, found the place he had left off and continued reading:

The title read – **Service:** *'While meditation can bring down power, service is the way of utilising that power for good. Failure to serve is like juggling more and more items in the air. If you do not pass them onto another you may well loose them all. In a similar way a dam will burst if it is overfilled with water.*

For service to be effective it is dependent on motive. When you are motivated to help your brother from the heart and you do this freely with the aim of giving without expecting anything in return, then you serve.

'Hands that help are holier than lips that pray.'

The act of serving is greater than the mere desire to serve'.

Pazamor closed the book, sat in his usual meditative posture and after saying 'The Great Invocation' pondered on whether meditation itself could be a service.

After what he had read of such things it seemed possible, but then he remembered a story Brother Benedict had told him about a missionary who became a recluse by retiring to a cave alone to meditate from sunrise to the midday and after one season literally blew his mind apart from too much energy stimulation.

Perhaps he could have avoided this if he had been able to share such energy in healing or like the Almoners, who give charitably to others, assisting the poor by giving leftover food or small amounts of money directly to those in most need. **'See the need and meet the need'.**

The next morning after a simple breakfast and water the friends continued on their way deeper into the forest. It was a cold start to the morning but a clear sky promised a warm day.

By mid morning they could see a small village up ahead.

Benedict was the first to comment on how quiet it seemed.

Duke motioned them to dismount while they approached the village. They could see no activity in front of them. Large mounds of earth stood erect, similar to what a giant mole might have left in its wake. There was also the stench of rotten flesh in the air surrounding them.

Duke asked Benedict and Pazamor to wait while he scouted on ahead.

On examining the mounds carefully he could see tunnels that were coated in green slime and were the width of a human shoulder span. He looked down one but could see little else, the stench making him repulse quickly from the opening.

On closer inspection of the village he noticed the remains of pig bones in the empty pens and outside one of the small huts he saw what looked like human bones. He did not think it necessary to check every hut, as the silence seemed to explain the fate of the villagers.

Duke motioned Benedict and Pazamor over to him and was about to explain what he had found, when something came whistling through the air and hit him hard in the stomach, nearly knocking him to the ground. If it had not been for the light armour he wore under his garments he could have been fatally wounded.

"Quick, get on the horses!" he shouted to Benedict and Pazamor, who did not need to question him. They all jumped onto their horses as quickly as they could, even Pazamor surprised himself with the speed at which he did this.

More missiles flew through the air – they were nuts, very hard nuts!

"Gallop to the east," shouted Duke, as he slapped Pazamor's horse hard on the backside and they all sped off in an easterly direction with Benedict leading the way.

Behind them they could see about twenty angry Wood Trolls screaming and spitting these hard nuts from their mouths like arrows fired from a bow.

The forest rained nuts as they rode away as fast as they could with the trolls running in hot pursuit.

Soon they approached a river with a heavy stone bridge over it and they hurtled across this as part of their escape route.

"We need to hide somewhere," shouted Duke, as they continued to race ahead, putting a little distance between themselves and the trolls.

"How about those caves up there?" shouted Benedict.

"Yes, good! Let's ride!"

Pazamor clung on for dear life. He had never ridden this fast before and his heart pounded with all the excitement.

As they reached the caves they could still see the trolls behind them crossing the bridge in hot pursuit. The horses came to stop just in front of the entrance and all quickly dismounted, venturing within the caves darkness before them.

Pazamor took out his green stone to light the way ahead and they walked deep within the ancient caves, guided by the dim light of the stone, held up high by Pazamor, who led the group.

The caves were cold and wet but thankfully they did not have to crouch, as there was ample head room. Symbols and pictures lined the inner walls. Pazamor reached for his compass to check they were heading in the right direction, mainly north from the old map he still had.

Benedict tried to read some of the signs on the walls but they were still travelling too fast to read them properly.

"Where are we?" asked Pazamor.

"These are the Caves of Bandor," answered Benedict.

"You must be joking Benedict. If that is so, we are entering the heart of the 'Thieves' Guild'," said Duke.

"Do you think the trolls are still following us?" asked Pazamor.

"I think they are the least of our worries Paz. The Guild will not take lightly to our rude entry into their world."

They continued onwards in a northerly direction until the symbols stopped and a large iron barred entrance stood in front of them.

"Halt! Who goes there and what is your business?" said a gruff voice from behind the door.

"We are Benedict, Duke and Pazamor on a mission to retrieve the Sorcerer's Sword. We are running from Wood Trolls.

There was a pause, the door swung open and they quickly entered, it locking behind them. But only just in time because following them was the trolls running and screaming and smashing into the heavy closed door in anger.

Before them lay a smaller door that was also locked. They were relieved to hear several bolts being slid across and it rise like a portcullis.

They were greeted by five dark-red cloaked figures, with crossbows pointing at them! However, the middle figure lowered their bow, stepped forward and dropped their hood.

A beautiful, young but rugged face met them.

"I am Katrina. My friends call me 'Cat'. I welcome you to our Guild but it is our tradition that you make a payment if you are to receive a safe passage through our halls," she demanded.

"We do not have anything of value," said Benedict.

"What of the green gemstone then?" said Katrina, pointing at Pazamor's neck.

Pazamor was reluctant to give it up, but knew that if he did not he would be putting his and his friend's lives at risk.

Katrina took the gem and held it up to the cave torchlight and noticed its green glow and the special symbols written within it.

"Have you shown the Brother?" she quizzed Pazamor.

Benedict was now more interested in the stone.

"No. Today is the first time Pazamor has displayed it in front of me. May I see it more closely?" asked Benedict, examining the stone. "The writing is Deva. Only a wizard can decipher it, but it does seem very familiar to me."

"Where did you get it Pazamor?" asked Katrina, "Only the cleric trolls are allowed such stones of power."

"It is from one such troll that I was given it."

"Given it? From a troll?" she spat on the ground. "They never give you anything. My parents were killed by Wood Trolls, the only thing I have had from trolls is trouble!"

The other four hooded thieves laughed in agreement.

"So you seek this Sorcerer's Sword do you? How is your quest progressing?" questioned Katrina further.

Pazamor was surprised at her question and was about to answer when Duke stood on his toe, as if to say, 'Be quiet!'

"We were on our way to Troll Tower to attempt to retrieve the magic gemstone that sits in the hilt of the sword, giving it its power. We discovered a village nearby in which all the inhabitants had been killed and then we were chased by Wood Trolls to these caves."

"That'll be the trolls then that killed the villagers, the ones that followed you," replied Katrina.

"No! Not this time," said Duke.

There was quiet.

"What do you mean?" asked Katrina.

"I mean it was not trolls that killed the villagers. I even believe that the same creature or creatures that killed the humans have also killed trolls and that we races are both being led to believe that one is responsible for the deaths of the other when in fact it is another race that is at fault."

"What are you talking about Sir?" asked Katrina in a surprised tone.

"You must have seen those mounds of earth appearing everywhere. It is my belief that the creature or creatures can tunnel and use this method of travel."

"The trolls have gone Mam," said one of the thieves.

"Well let us entertain our new friends," said Katrina in a loud demanding voice, - "a banquet!" she said, as she clapped her hands enthusiastically.

The other members of the Guild took the group to a spacious cave with a large fire in the centre of it, over which a black pot belly pig was placed to cook.

Entertainers jumped around, showing off their acrobatic skills, moving like shadows.

As the group sat down to watch, there was a loud crashing noise. Some of the Guild looked startled while others seemed to ignore it.

There was another resounding – "CRASH!" That was even louder than the first, and small stones dropped from the roof above.

A well armoured thief appeared and whispered something into Katrina's ear.

Katrina got up and left with ten other thieves, in the entrance, they were more heavily clad than usual.

"What is it Duke?" asked Pazamor.

"What do you think?" said Duke jumping to his feet, "what lives in caves and has the force to shake one. Come on, let's help!"

The three of them rushed off in the direction Katrina had left.

"CRASH!" Another smashing sound and as they went around the corner, one of the thieves came flying past them and into the wall with a "THUD!"

"It's broken through!" shouted another guard.

They could see two large grey Cave Trolls, – one with a tree trunk and beating the door in rage. The other picked up the fallen thief and crushed him to a pulp. The remaining thieves fired crossbow bolts as fast as they could, but could not penetrate the large Troll's thick skin and as such had little effect.

Behind the Cave Trolls stood the Wood Trolls they had seen earlier.

Duke took down one Cave Troll by hitting it in the leg joint with a crossbow bolts full force at point blank range.

Suddenly Benedict jumped up with unseen speed and took a small pole that he had been carrying on his shoulder. Tapping this on the floor twice made it extend to his own height, and he flew around the room smashing at the Wood Trolls and knocking them backwards.

One of the Cave Trolls was distracted by Benedict's speed and tried to squash him with the tree trunk, like you might try to squash a small fly with a stick.

The other was now having fun smashing at the door with its fists (having recovered from Duke's earlier attack).

Pazamor shouted to Katrina "Give me the stone and I can blind them with it!"

But Katrina was too busy dodging speeding nuts that were being spat out of the mouths of the Wood Trolls. A thief got in the way and was hit between the eyes by one such nut. He fell to the ground dead. Another nut narrowly missed Pazamor and embedded itself in the wall behind him.

Benedict however, had heard Pazamor say the words 'blind them!' He thought carefully, as he grabbed a small pouch from within his cloak, while still flying around the room with his staff, knocking the ricocheting nuts back towards the trolls who had fired them, knocking two of the beasts to the ground, dead from their own evil energy.

Benedict reached into the pouch and taking some fine magnesium dust threw it at one of the torches stuck to the wall.

"Close your eyes!" he shouted as the substance met with the fire.

"PHWEET! and then a massive flash of light that lit up the cave brighter than the light of day. The trolls screeched in agony and the Cave Troll that had been beating the door dropped the tree to hide its eyes with its hands and backed away from the bright light source, just before it went out.

The thieves and Pazamor's group quickly repositioned themselves as Benedict brought one of the large Cave Trolls to the ground by placing the pole behind its legs as it was retreating from the light. Tripping it landed with a large THUD! Before the trolls could recover and thrust another attack, Benedict quickly responded.

"Close your eyes again!" he shouted as he threw the last of the magnesium into a nearby torch and grabbed the torch which exploded into a bright light once again filling the cave. Benedict thrusted the torch forward at the trolls' eyes with one hand and with the other continued to batter at the trolls with breathtaking speed and agility.

The trolls had clearly had had enough by now. They screamed but could not see their assailant as they were blinded by the light. In panic a giant Cave Troll bolted down one of the cave's many tunnels.

The trolls that had not fallen left by way of the same passages, trying to exit the labyrinth of caves. The remaining Cave Troll limped away with a large wound inflicted by Duke, following its friend as quickly as it could and disappearing against the grey background of the walls of the passage.

Three Wood Trolls and three thieves lay dead with the wounded and dead being helped or dragged away. The remaining thieves and the group retreated behind the secondary doors and back to the banquet. Benedict offered his services in healing to those hurt in the fight and Katrina thanked him and allowed him to assist.

Duke, Pazamor and Katrina sat down to eat, while several other thieves with building skills left to repair the badly broken outer door.

Duke pulled a nut from his armour, it left a massive dent and a bruise on his skin, thankfully his armour had protected him against the deadly force.

Duke spoke first, breaking the solemn silence. "Does this happen very often?"

"Every now and again," responded Katrina, "though it is usually only one Cave Troll or a few Wood Trolls and not this many as today or to the death. Something must have stirred them to act in this way."

After finishing their meal Duke said they must continue on their journey to Troll Tower and Pazamor agreed.

"Troll Tower?" said Katrina in an interested voice, "that houses the magic gemstone which fits in the handle of the Sorcerer's Sword. It is said to be very powerful. Some people would pay a fortune for such a stone. Many traps protect it and you will need the sword's blade and hilt to make it work properly. Perhaps I should accompany you, with a couple of my men?"

Pazamor was about to say that it would not be necessary but Duke read the body language and quickly agreed with Katrina.

"Very well, I will go and prepare myself to leave," she left to get some other items.

"Pazamor, you do not refuse the Queen of Thieves, lest you end up like that!" said Duke pointing to some skulls hanging high from the ceiling. "Besides I think her skills will be of help to us in this task. She knows these forests better than any of us and she is easy on the eyes!"

Benedict returned.

"Are we off again?" said Benedict.

"It seems so," said Pazamor, "but we have others in our party," nodding towards Katrina and two thieves that were accompanying her (as she returned with horses for everyone).

"Come on then, let's go!" she spoke as if in charge of them all. Pazamor was about to mimic her actions when Duke again stood on his toes as if to say 'don't'.

"Ouch!" shouted Pazamor, "that really hurt!"

Duke looked at Pazamor as if to say – 'say nothing' but Pazamor looked crossly away from him.

"Is anything wrong?" spoke Katrina.

"Nothing Mam," said Duke, bowing courteously to her.

The group left through the main cave entrance, heading north towards Troll Tower.

Chapter 10
Troll Tower

The happy band crossed the stone bridge and headed north hugging the contours of the river. An hour into their journey Katrina beckoned them to slow their pace.

"There is a troll outpost nearby, we must tread more carefully," she said.

"I will scout on ahead," said Duke.

"Ok."

Pazamor, Benedict, Katrina and the other two guard thieves carried on north along the river, while Duke left his horse with them and headed in a north westerly direction alone.

Duke passed large trees that had been hollowed out with enough room to accommodate a wood troll. They did not live like humans but rather just stood in these spaces and merged with the tree itself, as if at one with it. If a troll was inside one such tree they were very difficult to spot, such was their transformation.

Duke looked very carefully but could only see empty holes in the tree trunks – it was as if no one was at home. He further examined the encampment. Large holes and mounds of earth lay nearby. Just as he had seen in the human encampment. While he could see no bones, plenty of broken branches were abundant – EKK! These branches were full of slime – they could very well be the remains of dead trolls. But what was killing the trolls and humans? Was it for food? What type of being could do this and leave little trace of itself?

Duke felt it wise to seek out the group instead of continuing on this trail and he found his way back to the river and ran north to catch up with his friends.

They were still contouring the river's edge in a northerly direction when he caught up with them.

"So what's up?" asked Pazamor.

Duke explained what he had seen.

"But for the trolls to attack us the way they did they must hold us responsible? Why would that be?" asked Katrina.

"We have been guilty of such crimes in the past Mam," replied Benedict, "why any different now?"

"Why can't we all just work together, be friends and share?" sighed Pazamor.

They all paused on that point and agreed that killing only seemed to bring about more killing: such was the wheel of life or 'Karma' as Benedict put it.

"The tower is still about a morning's travel through this thick forest which will be full of traps so this is why we must follow the river until the very last moment before entering," said Katrina.

After a short while the four of them were setting up camp by the river. None of them wished to get caught at night in Black Vintigan Forrest, for Wood Trolls would have a definite advantage over them, with their superior sight and smell. It is better to wait until morning.

Duke and the two guards set up camp. Katrina and Benedict talked together while Pazamor retrieved the battered small book and continued reading:

'Karma - *If you hit someone, expect to be hit back. If you steal from someone expect to be stolen from. If you love someone, you will be loved back. If you give freely, then freely shall you receive – this is the law of karma –* **'as you sow so shall you reap'.**

Complications seem to arise in this universal law when they extend over several life times. That is, the person in current incarnation is under the effects of a past incarnation. Examples could be when you meet someone in this life that seems awful to you for no apparent reason. It could well be in a past life you were bad to them. Here is where the apprentice must break the cycle.

Where you see hate give love, death – life, despair – hope. Only then will you eventually find balance in your life.

'Treat others as you would wish yourself treated' *and you will not go wrong.*

As to understanding whether this or that is karmic in nature it is better to just get on with life and the job of service – i.e. doing good to your brother, that way good will work out in your own life.

Let the Lords of Karma, your Master or soul work out the full effects of these lofty laws.

While man has his laws and criminals seem to often escape these laws, they cannot escape the universal law of karma. If the effects of karma are not dealt with in this lifetime, then the person will need to reincarnate (be born again) to the cycle of birth and death and put right their wrongs in their next life.

A man who stole from others but was never caught or brought to justice in this life, he died and was eventually reborn. In his next life he could not understand why his house was always being burgled or why his things went missing or were stolen from him …

After the group had eaten provisions supplied by Katrina, they settled down to sleep for the night.

When the morning came it was cold and misty, all the sun was hidden from view.

They prepared to leave camp after a quick drink of water and some bread.

"This bad weather is not a good omen," remarked Duke, as they walked slowly through the misty forest, their horses behind them and Katrina leading the way.

"I have not been this way for a while," she remarked, "It is a holy territory to the trolls. I have seen the Cleric Trolls performing rituals at the base of the tower. However, thanks to Pazamor's gift, she held up the green stone, examining it with great pleasure, I will expect to enter the tower and not have to stay outside.

Later, when they were deep in the forest, they heard the familiar sound of breaking branches. Pazamor could feel the hairs on the back of his neck standing on end, as if someone or something was watching him and his companions.

Visibility was still low with the thick mist surrounding them and to make matters worse the wind was picking up speed and it began to rain hard.

They put up their hoods to give some protection from the elements but the weather responded by increasing the downpour of rain and stronger winds battered them all as they fought further forward, the strong winds blew at the mist but it did not disappear, instead it hung around the forest as if it was stuck to it like glue.

Several trees they approached had holes in them, familiar to those used by trolls as homes. [Where humans, in the main, like to hide from the elements, trolls very much appreciate living at one with nature and would actually enjoy such bad weather!]

Duke looked around but thankfully saw no sign of the upturned earth or smell of rotten flesh he had discovered at the last troll camp he had visited.

The rain dripped from Pazamor's nose, like water from a cave's stalactite.

Everyone was already soaked through to the skin and morale was a little lower than usual, yet everyone was on heightened alert due to the dangerous territory they were passing through.

The trees in front of them moved in a disconcerting way. The branches were too low to ride their horses and so they dismounted and led them.

Pazamor knew they were being watched but not how to react, after all, it was they who were trespassing.

Suddenly Katrina motioned everyone to stop in their tracks and dive flat on the ground. A creaking noise could be heard in front of them and two massive logs on ropes of vine came crashing towards them. They swung over their heads but hit two of the horses, sending them flying into the air. The other horses bolted deep into the forest in a panic, taking all the provisions with them.

"It starts!" shouted Katrina, "run with me. Follow my steps exactly!"

She sped off ahead, the two guards and Benedict easily keeping up and accurately duplicating the steps she took. Duke also did well, however, Pazamor being at the back had slightly less luck and missed a stone and instead his foot came into contact with what looked like a giant mushroom.

The mushroom exploded into the air, letting off millions of tiny spores in a black vapour that engulfed Pazamor's throat and nostrils knocking him to the floor from the poison contained within. It all went dark.

When Pazamor awoke he found himself in what looked like a dungeon. He was hanging upside down from the feet, tied by vines, his hands also tied behind his back.

As he gently swung to and fro, he noticed, in the limited light, that the walls surrounding him were made of wood, indeed everything around seemed to be wooden. He tried to retrace his last steps in his mind but could only remember falling, after stepping on the giant mushroom.

Pazamor tried to assess the situation. He understood it likely that he was a prisoner of the trolls but what of his friends? He closed his eyes and tried to 'feel' the confines of the room. He was not alone, he could feel the presence of another and the energy felt neutral.

"Who's there?" whispered Pazamor.

"Onga, guard of Katrina, Queen of Thieves," came the hushed reply.

"Can you remember how we got here?" continued Pazamor.

"No, other than probably like you I missed a stone and stood on one of those blasted poisonous mushrooms! The poison doesn't normally kill but will render a human or large animal unconscious."

So what of the others, thought Pazamor as they hung there. And where are we?

*

After the fall of Pazamor and the guard the others were forced to continue running, aware of something behind them in close pursuit. They cleared the giant mushroom path and saw a forest clearing ahead of them.

The group felt uneasy about leaving Pazamor and another of their comrades behind, but knew that they had little choice, as to make a stand in this forest path would be certain suicide and what lay ahead was still as uncertain.

"We have to keep moving!" uttered Katrina, as if to reiterate these thoughts.

"Shh!" whispered Benedict, slowly taking his staff from his back. "We're still being followed and I sense a trap."

"I sense it too," replied Katrina.

Benedict brought the staff in front of him throwing it from hand to hand as they ran.

Katrina shouted at the guard – "You first!"

The thief looked a little worried but stepped up front by running even faster than the rest of the group, ducking and weaving as he ran to avoid being the target for potential arrows.

He just reached the opening when they all heard a large TWANG!

A door of spikes made of sharpened wooden staves met the thief, who tried to jump backwards, but couldn't avoid it in time and one of the spikes penetrated a hand as he put them out to stop his body hitting the door with its full force.

"Arrah!" he screamed, retracting a bloody hand.

Duke took his sword and smashed at the hinges of the door. Benedict, with one well placed aim of his staff to the middle of the door broke it in two and sent it flying out of their way.

They ran through the doorway into the open space of a large field. But this too was a trap.

Nuts from the surrounding forest trees rained down on them - they all ducked to the floor of long grass for cover, to avoid the deadly shower.

Benedict circled the group with breathtaking speed in a clockwise direction, batting the nuts with his staff, as he spun it in his hands as fast as he could.

To the untrained eye it looked as if Benedict had a large circular shield in front of him, such was the speed he could turn the staff with his hands. Any nuts hitting this were instantly repelled back to where they came.

Duke and Katrina scanned the area for a way out.

Did this happen the last time you were here shouted Duke?" above the whirring noise created by Benedict's rotating staff and the nuts 'dinging' off of this.

"It was night Duke, and no I was able to avoid all these traps. The way out is directly ahead," said Katrina, pointing at the forest wall of trees.

"But there's no entrance, only trees," replied Duke.

"Use your mind's eye, not your ordinary eyes!" said Benedict.

"Ahead, run!" shouted Katrina to them all.

They ran ahead following Katrina to what looked like a thick, impassable wall of trees.

As they avoided the last of the flying nuts they saw Katrina disappear directly in front of them through the trees. They all followed and were able to pass through what felt like a partial temporal projection of the woods, when in reality there was seemingly nothing but space in front of them.

Duke crossed his eyes and looked behind his eyes of seeing; he could detect the presence of the opening – but how did Katrina know? She did not have such skills – or did she?

"Intuition Duke, intuition, a good thief lives off it and I am one of the best," replied Katrina before Duke could ask her the question directly.

They continued to run on ahead following Katrina up a twisted wooden path, the trees around them different now, much smaller, twisted and gnarled.

"The trees!" shouted Benedict.

"Yes, they are alive. Trolls!" replied Katrina.

Slowly the branches moved and slits opened to reveal green eyes staring at them as they ran past.

"Quickly!" shouted Katrina, "up ahead." However, all they could see was another open field beyond with a giant tree stood in the middle, which extended far above the forest canopy above them.

"We are heading towards a giant tree?" Quizzed Duke, as they puffed and panted running as fast as their legs could carry them.

As they left the opening the remaining thief had his leg grabbed by a troll's hand and fell to the ground, the other trolls gathering around him like a pack of noisy dogs, their sharp teeth sinking into him, tearing him to pieces like a shoal of deadly piranha fish.

Duke, Benedict and Katrina crashed into the large tree in front of them. "We are trapped!" sighed Duke.

They all tried to catch their breath, while preparing to make a last stand.

"Give me a minute," said Katrina, examining the tree.

Cleric Trolls were approaching. Ten slowly approached from the entrance they had recently emerged from.

Katrina announced, "Found it!" both Benedict and Duke looked on in surprise.

Katrina had one hand on a part of the large trunk and took the green stone obtained from Pazamor. She thrust this into a small hole in the tree trunk and a door appeared, opening upwards in the middle of the trunk.

"Quickly!" she said.

Duke and Benedict did not need reminding a second time. With the Wood Trolls running towards them, they quickly entered. Katrina was the last to enter and as she removed the stone the trunk's door began to close. Duke noticed three similar stones on the inside of the tree wall, next to the trunk's entrance a green, yellow and a red stone.

He noticed the green stone was already pushed inwards.

Katrina was also looking, "Yes, of course!" she said, "these stones can act as keys! Quickly press the red one."

Before Duke could do so Benedict had already done so. They heard loud clicking sounds.

"Let's keep going – it must be upwards," whispered Katrina.

The trolls could not get to them, despite having their own green gem stones. None was of a high enough rank to possess a red stone and even the captain of their troop only had a yellow. It would take a high level cleric with a red stone or someone from the inside to open this door.

They carefully walked up a winding staircase and passed lots of wooden doors inside the tree on the way.

"Have any of us got an actual plan?" asked Duke smiling, as they continued to ascend the staircase.

"Yes," laughed Benedict, "retrieve the mystical stone and run like the wind!"

They all laughed, as best they could under the difficult circumstances.

A troll appeared from an entrance as they continued on their journey upwards. Duke fired a crossbow, the bolt hitting the door near the troll; it quickly went back inside, slamming the door shut.

Katrina was used to this lifestyle: living on the edge; living each day as if it were the last; maximising what you put in to get the most out.

They reached what seemed like the top – a wooden trap door in the ceiling, similar in design to the one they had seen in Fort Nomad.

Duke looked down the stairwell they had just climbed and could see far below another door set in the floor.

"I have a bad feeling about this," said Katrina.

Duke felt it too, but the group had travelled too far to turn back now.

Benedict opened the door above their heads with a sound, very different to the one he had used to open the one in Fort Nomad.

"What was that?" asked Duke.

"Troll language," replied Benedict.

"What did you say?" asked Pazamor.

"OPEN!" said Benedict smiling at them all.

A large chamber with holes in the walls letting in natural light greeted them. In the middle hanging from the ceiling, was a large silver concave mirror the size of a person in diameter.

Benedict stared in disbelief. Before they could do anything else a tall Wood Troll appeared, he was dressed in a white cloak and carried a staff with a stone on the top, similar in shape to the one retrieved by Katrina from Pazamor, except this one was coloured red.

The troll spoke in a tongue they did not understand and banged its staff on the floor. The room filled with a red mist.

Benedict spoke first. "Quickly cover your mouths!"

But it was too late; it was if the room span around and one by one the group fell to the floor unconscious from breathing in the strange red mist... it all went dark.

*

Benedict roused first to find himself in darkness, hanging upside down, bound from the feet with vines and hands lashed behind his back. He could hear light breathing nearby and could just make out the shape of Duke and Katrina either side of him.

Katrina gained consciousness next and moaned, "My head," trying to touch it with her hands but finding them tied.

Duke too slowly opened his eyes and struggled hard to free himself but also found himself too tightly bound.

For a short while there was silence while they contemplated how to free themselves.

"We are in a troll's dungeon," remarked Katrina, "I can see shackles on the walls and a closed entrance in front of us."

"What about above us?" asked Duke.

"I see a mechanism of some sort to raise and lower these vines tying us. There is a wheel on the wall. It could be our method of escape!"

"You can see all that!" remarked Duke.

"Duke, Katrina was born in the Caves of Bandor and moves like a cat in the night," explained Benedict.

"Yes, brother you are correct. This is one of the Guild of Thieves' specialised skills; as is escape!"

Katrina spun herself around on the vines and started swinging on them towards the wheel on the wall, just like a trapeze artist. She kept twisting and spinning and then reversed her spin while swinging to and fro.

The vines began to creak and stretch with all the movement. Katrina was very athletic but both Duke and

Benedict could only imagine the vine getting tighter. However, Katrina just kept twisting and turning. Then suddenly her hands were free.

Duke and Benedict stared at each other in the dim light.

Katrina managed to spin herself upwards so that she was actually standing on the vine with her full weight. She reached into her hair, removing the small dark wooden comb which helped keep her long, beautiful hair in a knot. Pulling this apart revealed a small knife, which she adeptly used to cut the vines holding her feet.

She set to work to free her friends. One by one they were free and had their feet on the floor.

"My bow!" said Duke in shock, after placing his hand behind his cloak and finding nothing.

They all checked for their valuable belongings but everything was missing, including the green gem stone.

Benedict lay on his back and asked the group to wait a moment.

While they waited, Benedict simply arose from his physical body and walked with his astral body through the door in front of them. As he traversed the dimensions he noticed that everything was covered in a golden glowing colour. Slowly he explored their surroundings, undetected by the trolls he passed. The door was locked from the outside and only a yellow or red gem would open it!

Benedict explored the other rooms on the same level by walking through the walls. He discovered Pazamor and another thief nearby.

Then he made an even more interesting discovery. In the middle of the hallway floor was a trap door with compass points. He carefully read the symbols, they were not in troll as he had expected but instead in Deva, the same as they had seen in Fort Nomad.

He touched the door – PHWEET! There was a fantastic flash of white light – Benedict's body jolted and all of a sudden he was back in the room with his friends.

He got up slowly.

"Are you ok?" asked Duke.

"A little light headed, but fine, thanks Duke. Right here is the situation: our doors are locked from the outside and only a yellow gemstone from a Captain of the Trolls or a red gemstone from a high cleric will open it. Pazamor and a guard thief are still alive and detained in a room opposite us. And, by the way, the door with entry to the magical gem stone is on this level – below ground!"

Duke laughed out loud, not being able to contain himself.

"I don't believe it! Pazamor has more lives than a cat. And we thought the mystical stone was held at the top of the tower! This Sorcerer's Sword must be of the earth, the pieces we have found so far are under it!"

Benedict laughed too, "Many a true word is spoken in jest Duke," he smiled.

"Benedict we need our weapons. Were you able to locate them?" asked Duke.

Benedict smiled, "No one asked me that," he said, "and I do not have enough etheric energy to make another projection today."

While they were pondering their next move, the High Cleric they had met earlier opened the door to their cell and entered, flanked by two heavily armoured troll guards each wearing a gold band around their heads with a yellow gemstone set near the ajna chakra area of the head.

Benedict, Duke and Katrina stepped back and took a defensive stance.

The High Cleric took another step forward on his own and spoke directly to Benedict and more slowly than before.

Benedict took some time and then replied in troll while both Duke and Katrina, looked on amazed.

Benedict asked about Pazamor and the Thief Guard. One of the Troll Guards left and soon came back with Pazamor and the Thief Guard, pushing them towards their friends.

The High Cleric was quiet and looked at them all. Then he spoke.

Benedict translated to the group: "We must pick one from us to take the troll tests. If they succeed we may take the gem and go free. If we fail, then our fate is sealed!"

The troll spoke again:

"We have but a short time to decide which of us will take the challenge," translated Benedict as clearly as he could.

The trolls left the room and there was silence. Then the other Troll Guard returned with all their items including the green gemstone which it handed to Pazamor.

Pazamor looked again, it was the same troll he had seen in his village, the one he had helped to save, who had given him the green gemstone in the first place.

Pazamor touched his hand as if to say thanks. The troll touched Pazamor's hand with his other, also as a gesture of friendship.

"Thank you," said Pazamor.

The troll said something and then left the group alone.

"So you got your stone back then Paz, said Duke, patting him on the shoulder in friendship.

Pazamor smiled, "Yes Duke," he said.

"The Universal Spirit returns to us what is rightfully ours - if we are patient," added Benedict.

"Oh rubbish!" said Katrina as she snatched the stone from Pazamor's hand, as he was admiring it and before he could place it back safely in his pocket.

"'The Universal Spirit helps those that help themselves and *take what you can today for it may not be there tomorrow!'* at least that is what we thieves say," said Katrina.

"Ouch! She dropped the gem on the floor. "It burnt me!" She winced, pointing at the green gem in front of them.

Let me take a closer look at that stone said Benedict, carefully picking it up.

Then Benedict sounded a note not unlike the OM – OMMMMMM…" louder and louder, longer and longer he held the note. The gemstone transformed colour before their eyes – turning a bright yellow and glowing even brighter than the green it had been.

Benedict handed the stone back to Pazamor. "I think you will find this even more powerful now. Though with this power comes more responsibility."

"What did you do?" asked Pazamor.

"With the power of sound I changed the stone's vibrational rate. You could say the stone took an initiation and passed!"

"Well, which of us is to take the challenge?" asked Duke.

"I will!" voiced Katrina, stepping forward, "you will need a women's intuition to pass this test!"

Benedict wasn't so sure. "Young Paz has those qualities also," he said.

"But Katrina is best at escape," mentioned Duke, in her defence.

"What do you think?" asked Katrina, starring directly at Pazamor.

"I think that if you believe in yourself this much then you will succeed but if your heart is placed only on greed then this mystical gem will not only burn you but also consume you."

"Pazamor has a point," responded Duke. "Our first choice would have been Sapphira but as she is not here, such a task has fallen to Pazamor, he has got us thus far."

"All right! All right!" said Katrina, "I will get this mystical gem for you but in return I ask of you a trade. The yellow gem stone!" pointing at the stone in Pazamor's hand.

"And what will you do with it?" asked Benedict, "you saw what it did to you when it was green – and now it is yellow and twice as powerful.

"I will wear it around my neck and form a peaceful alliance between my people and theirs."

There was silence for a moment.

"You would do that? asked Benedict in a surprised tone.

"Yes, we thieves have lived in the caves for too long now. It is time we shared them and the trolls shared their forest with us."

Pazamor placed his hand on Katrina's, as did the rest of the group.

"We trust in you Katrina. Go with our love and succeed, because the Universal Spirit is within you, as it is in us all," spoke Pazamor.

"I will prepare," she said and started practising her moves while Benedict and Duke sat down to meditate on the shield of prayer which is a protective mantra prayer that would surround Katrina while she engaged on the tasks ahead. The other thief assisted Katrina in her warm-up exercises.

Pazamor looked into his pocket – his book was still there – he sat in a corner and began to read once again:

'Secret forces are bringing compatible spirits together. If the man permits himself to be led by this ineffable attraction, good fortune will come his way.

When deep friendships exist, formalities and elaborate preparations are not necessary.'

The power of true friendship should never be underestimated, for in it is true love. When one is ready to give up so much as to die for another then in such giving up will you receive as much of the spirit.

'Wherever there are two or more gathered in my name there shall I be.'

Pazamor put his book away and sat with the others.

Benedict instructed them on the necessary means of prayer protection, with the target being Katrina and how the three of them could make a triangular force, increasing the power of the prayer they were sending forth.

Shortly the High Cleric Troll returned.

"Who have you chosen?" he asked Benedict, who immediately translated for the others.

Katrina stood forward.

"I will take the challenge!" she said boldly.

The High Cleric Troll took Katrina out of the cell and towards the centre of the hallway to the trap door in the earthen floor, just as Benedict had seen and described to them earlier.

The troll held its staff high in the air and chanted. The red stone on his staff shone brighter and the trap door rose and was held there by the continuous notes sounded through his throat chakra.

He motioned to Katrina to enter.

She took the yellow gemstone, that had been green, to help light her way in the corridor before her. It was damp, dark and cold down there and she could hear an underground river in the distance beyond the dripping water from stalactites above her head.

She heard the door above crash down into place and felt very alone, a feeling she had become accustomed to in life.

Chapter 11
A Walk through the Woods

Sapphira continued on her journey east, with Haddon by her side flitting up and down in the air like a large butterfly. As she walked slowly but purposefully through the open land, small plants brushed at her feet. The air was warm and the sun bright. Sapphira took a small glass vial from her belt, sipped the contents and felt refreshed.

Eventually Sapphira and Haddon came across a hamlet. Sapphira slowed and Haddon followed in her actions. About thirty paces away stood a small country cottage which looked of human origin. Sapphira motioned Haddon to go on ahead and see what lay before them. While she waited, Sapphira sat and munched slowly and quietly on some provisions. After a very short time Haddon returned.

"So, what is up ahead then?" asked Sapphira.

"An old lady, living on her own I believe," said Haddon.

"It sounds harmful enough," Sapphira mumbled to herself. "Ok, let's go ..."

Sapphira and Haddon arrived at a beautifully kept thatched cottage. Red and pink roses adorned the sides of the path to the door, their fragrance wafting through the air. The path they walked on was made of large flat stones sunk into the floor that wove in and out of the large flower, herb and vegetable garden surrounding the building.

Sapphira knocked at the door.

"Who is it?" asked an elderly voice from behind the door.

"Sapphira," responded Sapphira.

"And your friend, who or what is that?"

Sapphira was surprised that the old women could see Haddon – as he would be invisible to most, just like the Masters, ghosts and Devas of the world.

Haddon laughed and ran circles around the head of the old women.

"Get off me! Get off!" she screamed, "he is worse than a child!" the old women spluttered, after trying to knock Haddon out of the air with a broken broom.

"What do you want? she asked.

"We are just passing through," responded Sapphira.

"My name is Belinda," replied the old lady.

Sapphira lifted her eyebrows in surprise.

"Yes, I know you were going to ask me my name, some people around these parts call me a witch! What do you think?"

Sapphira was more on her guard now. She noticed that the women had long white hair, a pointed nose, was blind in one eye, the other being black. Yes, she could well be a witch!"

Belinda laughed confidently as if she had worked out a puzzle, "You are very quiet for a Sorceress. What is your real business here?"

"As I said, we are just passing through."

"Well, sit down by my cauldron dear, I will make you some warm food."

"Thank you. That would be very welcoming."

They both sat around a large black cauldron in the middle of the room which was bubbling and boiling away – whatever it was, it smelt wonderful!

"I do not mean to offend you Belinda but I do not eat meat or eggs."

Belinda laughed again, "Oh, that's alright dear – neither do I. Have you seen my garden?"

True, from what Sapphira had seen of the garden there was no livestock – only vegetables, fruits and herbs.

"I was once as pretty as you."

"Pardon me?" said Sapphira, with Haddon buzzing around the cauldron trying to work out what was within.

"I was once as pretty as you," repeated Belinda but I got so immersed in the world of magic that I became lost in it.

Instead of me controlling the spirits that I conjured they controlled me. Two beings like your friend here had me eating grass like a goat and barking like a dog for about two summers. I was as mad as a pixie until a friendly wizard by the name of Torrum passed by and banished the evil spirits back to their domain."

At this point, Sapphira pricked her ears, "My Master!" she said.

"Mine too!" said the old lady, smiling.

"It is hard living out here on your own Sapphira, especially in the winter time, when the ground turns white and is as hard as rock but then my magic is useful," she smiled.

"I guess I have been more fortunate," replied Sapphira, "My father died of disease when I was only four summers old and my mother died of starvation when I was nine. If it were not for the kindness of Torrum taking me in then I am not sure where or what I would be doing now – or even if I would be alive. So is the soup ready?"

"Ask your friend," motioned Belinda.

They both looked at Haddon who had decided the soup looked like a good place to have a bath and was dripping wet with a leek hanging from his head.

Belinda closed her eyes and hummed a note, next she threw her hands towards Haddon, as if throwing a stone. A small golden ball of light blasted forth and hit Haddon with full force, sending etheric sparks flying in the room. They all laughed, including Haddon, who seemed intoxicated by the extra energy.

"Feisty little thing isn't he?" said Belinda.

"He has been with me a couple of sunrises now, I will be sorry to see him go."

"Are you getting attached to him? Like ... like you love him?" Belinda said with a friendly smile.

"I guess so Belinda."

"Not a bad thing, but there are different types of love, as I'm sure you know. You need to be careful with what we call 'love'. If it is from the heart chakra, then you can't usually go wrong, but when the head gets involved as well – it can turn to 'attachment' or 'possession' and like a bar of soap, if you hold it too tightly, it will fly out of your hands. Rather take it slowly and gently. Be detached, not cold but neither boiling hot. Find a balance in life." Belinda sighed. "Listen to me, you are so young – just take life slowly, but still live it to the full – ***love is giving and forgiving***.

Share with all you meet and I think you will have a good life."

"You are very wise," responded Sapphira.

"Well age matures one, hopefully we get wiser as we get older," replied Belinda smiling from the heart.

They sipped the hot vegetable soup. Haddon fell asleep and as he did so he blipped in a flash of light and disappeared from view.

Sapphira looked on.

"He will be back again. He is tied to your consciousness," said Belinda.

"Yes, I know, it's just that the path of the wizard can be a lonely one."

After eating the soup, Belinda talked some more with her guest, sharing some spells and old stories.

It's getting late so you may sleep here for the night. I can make a bed of hay and you can have your own room.

"Wow! Thanks. It beats sleeping outside again Belinda."

Sapphira slept well and left early the next morning with Port Kepland about a day's travel away.

Belinda gave Sapphira some provisions and rare herbs for more exotic spells. The two hugged and wished each other luck on the path of life.

Sapphira continued walking through the forest, on a well trodden path. It was very peaceful, birds could be heard singing in the trees while a small field mouse ran in front of her stopping now and again to eat a piece of corn. Above a buzzard circled, expecting to catch the mouse but letting it go because of Sapphira's presence. The mouse seemed to wink its small black eye and then disappeared into the undergrowth.

Sapphira smiled and continued to walk along the path, passing a small wood ant mound. The ants were busily moving through the forest floor carrying green leaves to their nest. They marched with such purpose and strength. A bumble bee buzzed from flower to flower, gathering what nectar it could and rewarding the flowers for their sweet food by transferring pollen.

Sapphira wondered on what life might be like if she were married with a family. She had heard from her Master that if one was in a relationship then such sexual relations would reduce and dissipate one's own spiritual power bringing it down to the Sacral and Base Chakras. Indeed the same was true if one had a family for one's focus would also be divided amongst family members. To keep one's focus on the Universal Spirit and at the ajna chakra all the time, was not at all easy, especially with the many distractions provided by life.

Sapphira once again concentrated on her ajna chakra as she walked, going over the many magical symbols and spells her Master had made her memorize in her mind's eye. She saw these shapes all around her, just like some flower petals are shaped as pentagons and ferns as fractals – she saw shapes and power in everything.

When she crossed her eyes and changed her focus slightly she could also see a very different world of colours and shapes - the astral world of the Deva.

At this moment that world was full of beautiful colours and at peace.

She continued to walk, small fairies from the Deva Kingdom buzzed by, their wings making the same sound as a large bumble bee. Sapphira took a couple of micro flasks and some earth. She threw the micro flasks into the air with one hand and a handful of earth with the other, while making several incantations. There was a flash of light and Haddon was back.

"Good morning miss!" shouted Haddon.

"Have you been busy my little friend?"

"Just fixing some good people's gardens and having fun," he said with a wicked smile.

They continued on the path a bit longer, when Sapphira came across a large tree trunk that had been cut by village peasants. She carefully examined the bark – it was a great oak – perfect she thought. This is something that actually gives you energy rather than takes it from you.

She sat cross-legged on it.   Haddon understood and instantly created a fire for Sapphira.

"Thank you Haddon," responded Sapphira as she grabbed a small pouch from her belt, and removed some food fashioned into the shape of small cubes, supplying concentrated life giving energy.

Sapphira boiled some water with a few herbs placed within it over the fire. She also took a small clear spherical crystal and threw this into the burning embers. Shadows danced within the small ball as Sapphira concentrated on an image of Torrum and utilised her ajna chakra to send a message telepathically to Torrum's throat chakra, by briefly seeing him and his throat chakra in her mind's eye.

A loose image of Torrum appeared inside the ball. "How are things progressing Sapphira?" he asked.

"I hope to reach Port Kepland by night fall," she answered, "and I will locate the Jack Rabbit once there."

"Good, but do avoid the graveyards at night. See you soon!"

There was a flash of light and the image was gone. Sapphira grabbed the ball from the fire without burning her hand and placed it back in its pouch. She closed her eyes concentrated on her ajna chakra, sounded a short mantra and meditated for a while.

It was time to move on again. She picked up her belongings and once again she and Haddon traversed the dirt track of an open path. Soon they entered a forested area again.

A short distance within and the sound of wood being chopped could be heard. Up ahead was a tall forester, cutting a fallen tree with an axe.

"Hello," he said, as Sapphira approached, pushing his long black hair aside from his large brown eyes. He was unshaven and had the strong smell of trees and earth, or at least she thought it was earth.

For this reason alone, Sapphira kept her distance. "Hello," she responded, "it is a good day for chopping wood."

"Indeed, my house will benefit from this," he replied. "I need it to build a fence around my farm. Wild pigs came a few sunrises ago and ate all my crops. I now have nothing to eat. I have to start all over again," he said in a depressed voice.

"Perhaps I could help," said Sapphira genuinely.

The forester laughed, "Unless you are rich or a magician, I doubt it pretty lady."

"Well, it depends on your definition of 'rich' if you mean an abundance of coins or gold then no, but if you mean in happiness and love then yes. As to being a magician? Let us put it to the test, shall we?"

The forester gathered the wood and placed it on the back of a donkey, tethered nearby. They travelled off the path and deeper into the woods. Soon they arrived at a badly built wooden house, which was more like a small hut than anything else.

Sure enough, crops of corn lay decimated before them. Sapphira pondered for a moment then looked at the remaining seeds of corn which lay scattered before them. She spoke to Haddon, who the forester couldn't see, and instructed him to plant all the seeds he could find, while she kept back one for herself.

Haddon planted them all in less time than it takes to boil water. In which time Sapphira was making incantations towards the weather. She took a micro flask of water and smashed it, releasing the water on to the seed in her hand. As she did this, rain clouds gathered and it became dark all around them.

The forester just stared in disbelief and then as thunder and lightning appeared he ran for the cover of his small hut, bending down and peering out of the hole in the wooden wall – which was an excuse for a window.

The thunder clapped and the sky flashed white, while the rain poured down all around them.

Sapphira continued to make incantations and the seed in her hand split open, and the ground in front of them seemed to move.

Slowly the seed in her hand grew and as it did Haddon rushed around the seeds he had planted – small shoots beginning to grow up before them in the ground, mirroring the growth of the seed in her hand.

The forester looked on in awe.

Within a very short time the entire field was covered in freshly grown corn.

Sapphira approached the forester and handed him the piece of corn in her hand. The forester quickly placed it on a table and touched it to see if it was real. Next he ran into the field and did the same with another piece and then another piece...

"Thank the Universal Spirit!" he shouted at the top of his voice on his knees and looking up to the sky.

"Thank you very much!" he said, shaking Sapphira's hand in animated joy.

Sapphira couldn't help but smile from the heart and share in the man's new found happiness and joy.

After the initial excitement he wanted to give something back that would be of help to Sapphira, though he had very few worldly goods.

"So what brings you through Woodville Wood?" asked the forester.

"I seek a part of the Sorcerer's Sword for our group, to help defeat the evil wizard Kraytos and his many demons.

"Would that be anything to do with these strange looking ant-like mounds," pointing behind the hut at several large holes.

"Yes, indeed it is," replied Sapphira.

"Ugly looking beasts, but at least they got rid of my wild pig problem!"

"You mean they ate all the wild pigs in the forest?"

"Yes, the noise from the dying pigs was horrible and lasted for two sunrises. The monsters look like they are made of rock and have large ears that cover their faces. As they seem to travel underground it must protect their eyes and face. I think their tunnels are made by secreting slime from their skin."

"Corrosive acid!" said Sapphira in interest.

"Well I guess, as the slime they produce burnt my hand," he lifted a hand to show a large scar on his left wrist. The other interesting thing is that they only come out of the tunnels at night."

"Have you discovered any weaknesses?" she asked with raised eyebrows.

"Well, I am not sure, but a vat of vinegar I had which I threw down one hole to get rid of the disgusting smell produced a horrendous scream and smoke from this. It was like no scream I have heard before."

"Do you have any vinegar left?"

"Yes, a complete barrel."

Sapphira placed some of the vinegar in several micro flasks around her leather belt and took a drop in a wooden cup. Pouring it near one such entrance she noted a chemical reaction – of course! The vinegar is neutralising the acid. It must have really hurt the Kraytos Demons if they secrete acid from their bodies, it could really burn them, possibly destroy them.

'We might not need the Sorcerer's Sword after all', she thought to herself.

Chapter 12
The Magic Gem

The cold cave walls flickered with shadows as the dim yellow light of the gemstone lit the way ahead for Katrina. She passed large cobwebs, undisturbed for many summers until now. The floor crunched under her feet, the sound of small shells breaking under the impact as she progressed. There were puddles of water here and there and the noise of a fast flowing river grew louder as she cautiously moved deeper into the cave.

Bats fluttered past Katrina animated by moths that had come to investigate the yellow light around her. It was to prove their last investigation as the bats made a tasty meal of them before the spiders could.

It felt slightly claustrophobic down here, the quietness closed around her like a blanket. She could hear her breathing and heart beating fast but other than that, just another underground cave. Thoughts raced through her head: What were the tests? Where was the Sorcerer's Stone?

As she advanced further the cave walls began to glisten with fissures of gold showing through. Then she thought she heard the loud roar of a Cave Troll up ahead. It had probably caught her scent, or the noise of the bats had disturbed it. Either way, it was moving towards her very fast.

The underground river was now in view directly in front of her. It flowed through yet another underground cavern. To the left and right of this were smaller caves. The Cave Troll could be heard from the right.

Katrina was faced with four choices, return the way she had come, turn left, turn right and face the beast or jump into the river to possible deeper danger.

She hesitated for a moment to catch her breath, then dived into the fast flowing river in front of her.

Katrina put out her hands to try and protect her head from hitting the rocks, while she was twisted and turned in all directions under the fast flowing river.

It felt like an eternity, but was probably only a very short space of time.

She emerged into a large underground lake. The water was actually shallow enough to stand, but deep enough to reach the level of her neck.

She carefully held up the yellow gem stone from around her neck. It lit up the cave like a full moon's reflection on a lake. Thousands of clear stalactites from the cave roof glistened and bounced the light back off the lime stone walls.

On these walls were symbols, again ancient, and again probably Deva.

The only problem being, Katrina didn't read Deva well. Wizards were best at such languages, followed by the monks, but thieves were a poor third choice.

Still, she was the one here now and would have to be the one to try and understand them.

Eventually she found some pictures depicting five cave exits with what looked like stalactites falling from the cave ceiling – these looked very sharp and you didn't need to be a genius to work out what would happen if you took the wrong exit. She continued to examine the pictures and symbols.

The next picture showed seven large stalactites with lots of small clusters at the bottom of the picture of a cave with an entrance opposite the seventh in the middle of the cave wall.

The next picture had broken away from the cave wall and could not be deciphered.

Katrina held her breath and concentrated hard again on the pictures before making her way through the water to the front of the cave. As she waded she felt the water receding. Still, the cave glistened as she moved through it, holding the yellow glowing gem before her.

Then, in front of her were five identical cave exits. At this point the water was at knee height. She found herself beginning to shiver from the cold as she pondered on which exit to take. Each of the exits had a wooden door covering them, above these were many sharp pointed stalactites, just as she had seen in the cave picture earlier.

Gut instinct told her to take the middle door of the five, though she was not sure why.

She stopped in her tracks as she noticed small stalagmites forming in front of her feet and her senses told her something was wrong!

Katrina trod more carefully, avoiding as best she could the now many stalagmites amongst her feet. The water level had dropped below her knees and she could feel a slight crunching under her feet from standing on thousands of small shells. The five cave-like openings were now about five paces away.

'Click!' one of the stalagmites in front of her broke. Katrina dived to her left, just as a large stalactite above her came crashing down where she had stood before and embedded itself in the ground.

However, while diving to the left she had broken another stalagmite. She didn't hang around. Making a spinning leap in the air she just avoided another large stalactite crashing to the ground narrowly missing her.

She continued to run and leap, while large stalactites fell from the roof of the cave like giant daggers. As they hit the floor they shattered into thousands of pieces, and were thrown into the air once more, some of which cut her arms and face.

Katrina reached the middle entrance with a running leap, a roll and a kick, knocking the wooden door down and quickly passing through it and catching her breath again as she hit the ground.

As she walked through the cave's corridor she flapped her arms to remain warm and stop shivering. The yellow light from the stone still helped in illuminating the way ahead.

At the end of the corridor was a large open cave space, but below what seemed like a bottomless pit.

In front, just like the cave painting she had seen earlier, was a large stalactite but only space stood between the crevice she was on and this large rock in front of her.

Katrina quickly tied a small grappling hook to her belt that was around her waist, she unwound this several times to produce a makeshift rope.

She threw the hook so that it wrapped around the stalactite in front of her and with the other arm pushed a small button on her left wrist, releasing a spring and a three pronged claw.

Katrina swung across the chasm and as she did she could see another such stalagmite in front, while below she could see nothing but darkness.

A cold wind echoed in her ears, the cave was very eerie. A few bats also fluttered above her, nearly making her lose balance.

As she swung to the next stalactite she utilised the claw to hold on while she released the grappling hook from the other and threw it to the next stalactite.

Katrina reached the other side with ease but needed to stop for some provisions to recover her energy level.

After a short break she continued along yet another long corridor. Eventually it opened up, and on her right was … Wait a minute… this sight looked very familiar. It was the underground river she had entered earlier. She had travelled in a circle!

But where was the magical stone?

Katrina sat down puzzled but then noticed something strange about the existing stone she had – it was a little larger and had another two symbols on it.

Behind her she could hear the noise a Cave Troll [unbeknown to her it lived at the bottom of the cave she had just traversed and it had climbed up the stalagmites and leapt across to the entrance, following the noise made by Katrina when crossing the cave].

She had three choices: go down the last cave corridor, go back to her friends, empty handed or stay and fight! [One of Duke's favourite options].

The Cave Troll was in view now. Katrina panicked and ran back the way that led to the exit. The Cave Troll, roaring like a mountain gorilla, ran in hot pursuit of its prey.

As Katrina raced back up the damp cave floor she slipped and before she could get up the Cave Troll was on top of her.

It was massive and filled the small corridor with its large body mass.

However, as it grabbed her, lifting her in its large arms, and about to crush the life force out of her, she thought of Duke and her other new friends in her mind's eye. As she did so time and space shimmered around her. Although the troll had managed to grab her it was as if it was holding a slippery fish and Katrina managed to escape through its arms and continued back up to the trap door before it could realise what had happened. She quickly opened it to escape and then closed it again to avoid the monster catching her.

Standing before her were the Troll Cleric and two guards. He motioned a guard to leave. The cleric held out its hand to Katrina.

Katrina hesitated but gave the troll the only gemstone she had, her eyes lowered to the floor as if in defeat and worried that she could have fatally let her friends down.

The guard returned with Benedict.

The High Cleric spoke directly to Katrina in troll. It gave the yellow gem stone back to her.

Benedict translated. "Hold the yellow stone before you."

Katrina did as instructed.

The High Cleric took his staff and touched the stone, chanting some words of magic.

Before their eyes the stone changed from yellow to red.

"You now have before you a sorcerer's stone and this may be used with the Sorcerer's Sword. You and your friends may go free and unhindered by the Wood Troll kingdom.

The guard let go of Benedict and they were all reunited before bidding farewell to the High Cleric and leaving Troll Tower.

"Can you do that Benedict?" asked Katrina, referring to changing a stone from yellow to red.

"No, only the Abbot could do that," remarked Benedict.

Katrina said farewells to Benedict and Pazamor and gave Duke a big kiss on the lips. Pazamor and Benedict looked up at the sky as if pretending not to notice anything.

"Look me up some time soon," she said and ran her hand down his chest and up his neck, touching his lips with two fingers and starring into his eyes tantalisingly.

Duke just stared mesmerised. He definitely liked Katrina but didn't know she shared the same feelings – until now.

"It's a nice day to travel to Port Kepland," said Pazamor to Benedict, breaking the silence.

Katrina smiled and gave the red stone to Pazamor. "What of your need for the stone to forge a peace between your people and the trolls?" asked Pazamor.

"You have made me realise that I do not need these material things, that friendship is more valuable than gold and that we can find peace through love. Good luck." She ran into the forest, quickly disappearing from view as quietly as a shadow.

Duke's eyes followed her.

"She's a nice person, isn't she Duke?" said Pazamor.

"That she is Paz, that she is," said Duke with a deep sigh.

Duke had a bigger smile on his face than the rest of the group and seemed a little distant in his thoughts.

"Well to Port Kepland then my friends," said Benedict, "Sapphira is much closer to us now, I can feel her energy."

They continued on their way with Port Kepland in the distance.

Chapter 13
Port Kepland

The party of three had been travelling for half a day when they reached the edge of the River Raven.

"We will need to attract the attention of a boat if we are to cross to Port Kepland," suggested Duke.

"Will that do? asked Pazamor pointing to a small wooden pier that extended about fifteen paces into the water.

The three continued to walk towards the pier, across it and over the river.

"A pity they don't have a bridge!" sighed Duke.

"It is a bit too far for that Duke," explained Benedict.

Both Pazamor and Duke laughed.

"I was only joking Benedict! There must be a flag or something nearby."

Pazamor found the flag Duke was looking for next to a sign which suggested the cost of crossing was 3 danks each.

Duke and Pazamor looked at Benedict, whose turn it was to laugh now.

"Yes, I have enough money for me," said Benedict with a smirk on his face.

Duke and Pazamor looked at each other as if to say, 'have we upset him?'

"Oh, I am only joking," said Benedict, "I have enough money for us all," smiling.

Benedict sat down against a wooden post closed his eyes and after making what looked like the sign of the cross, except that he touched his eyes instead of his shoulders when making this, started to meditate.

Duke picked up the orange flag and started waving to a boat in the distance. Pazamor sat down, got out his tattered book and began to read again:

'Most of us are lost in a false world of 'ego'. We believe us to be something we are not – like a king that thinks he is above his people or a peasant who thinks that he is below his king – both are sides of the same coin. If we think highly or lowly of ourselves it is of the ego.

*Far better to be 'detached' from life not cold and uncaring or so caring that one can do nothing because one is lost in sadness. It is better to be detached – this is when one is **in the world but not of it**.*

Things do not control us – we are in control of them. The winds of life's troubles do not blow us about, for we are like the light of the sun in their presence.

It is not right that we think of ourselves above or below another, rather that we as beings, 'just be!'

Ego can be eradicated through 'service' which is giving or helping from the heart, without seeking any reward.'

"The boat has responded!" shouted Duke.

They are still some way off though Duke," said Benedict, still in his meditative posture.

Pazamor however had closed his book and was excitedly looking on. He had never seen such a large ship before.

"It is fast!" said Pazamor.

"Hummn... a bit too fast Paz," murmured Duke.

"What flag does it have?" asked Benedict.

Pazamor strained to see, "I think it is black."

"Black!" said Duke and Benedict in unison.

"Are you sure?" asked Benedict now coming out of his meditation and Duke stopped waving his flag, acting more cautiously.

"I can't see any flag," said Benedict, "are you absolutely sure about what you have seen Pazamor?"

"Yes, they have just lowered it. I think it had some white in it as well but I'm not absolutely sure of that. What is up Ben? .... Duke?"

"It could be pirates Paz," said Duke looking across to Benedict. "They are known to operate in these waters."

"Run for cover!" shouted Duke. The three of them ran to the woods and hid from view behind some trees and thick undergrowth.

"Are they still coming towards us?"

"Yes - no wait a minute, they are turning back."

"Opportunists!" said Benedict, "well spotted Paz."

"You could have saved us being taken. Such ships don't stop at press ganging anyone they come across into their service and failure to comply can result in a jump overboard," responded Duke.

"What do we do now Duke?" enquired Pazamor.

"Well you can swim across if you want Paz but I think we should make some canoes or a raft."

Benedict looked at Duke, "We could lose another day!"

"Then we better work together on this."

"There is another way Duke," announced Benedict.

"Let us camp here for the night and I will get a message to Sapphira, she should be in Port Kepland by now," said Benedict.

Under the cover of the forest, though close to the river, they started to settle for the night.

Benedict prepared his cooking utensils, while Duke started on the fire and also collected branches for his raft. Pazamor went foraging as he fancied getting some limpets from the shoreline, as the sea joined the river at this point and the water had an amount of salt in it, supporting such life and sea fish.

He decided he would have to wait for the cover of darkness before obtaining them so instead climbed a tree and utilised his good eyesight to pick out all the large rocks on the beachhead that would support limpets. He noticed that the sea was coming in and the level rising – this didn't help matters.

In the meantime he carefully looked around at the plants available. Some large dandelion leaves would make a good wild lettuce he thought and some stinging nettles, which he carefully picked, a good nettle tea.

Pazamor passed the ingredients to Benedict, whom already had some water boiling, from a fire started by Duke. He then went to collect the limpets with further help from Duke. After a short time they had enough and returned to the camp fire to warm nettle tea, while Benedict cooked the main course.

"So what is Sapphira *really* like then Duke?" asked Pazamor.

Duke smiled, "Do I detect a sense of admiration for someone here?" He said.

Pazamor went a bright red, "Well you know her better than me," he responded.

The space around Duke shimmered like the sun's heat on a sun baked path.

"It is better to make your own mind up with people you meet in life and not let others make it up for you. See the positive side of all people and remark on it. Do not

participate in idle gossip, for this is often a poison, and those that gossip with you will often gossip about you.

Speak good of all. Even your enemies can provide a challenge to you in bringing forth more good."

The shimmer was gone and Benedict broke a temporary silence... "More nettle tea Paz?"

Pazamor snapped out of it. "Oh thanks Ben."

"I will bid goodnight and hope to contact Sapphira," spoke Benedict in a quiet tone, before lying on his back to astrally project himself to Sapphira.

A short time passed with Pazamor and Duke talking quietly amongst themselves when Benedict's body jolted and he sat up. He turned to Duke and said, "You need to stop thinking of Katrina so much, Sapphira has been trying to contact you telepathically but you have been blocked.

Duke's face went a bright red colour but in the fading light this would have been difficult to see.

Pazamor laughed and said, "Your focus is at your solar plexus Duke, not your ajna chakra."

Duke responded, "Shut it Pazamor, your focus will be in your bum with my boot!" he said playfully, kicking Pazamor up the backside with his foot.

They all laughed.

"On a serious note friends, Sapphira is aware that a pirate ship we saw earlier is still present and a small boat from this will soon row towards us with the aim of capture."

Duke listened intently, "This is good!" he said, "I have a plan."

Pazamor and Benedict both looked at each other in surprise at what Duke was saying.

"Please share," said Benedict.

"We keep the camp fire burning and make out that we are asleep, take their boat and row to Port Kepland.

"What about the pirate ship?" asked Pazamor. "It can outrun a small rowing boat and would probably smash us into the water when we sail past it."

"Not if we create a diversion," said Benedict. "Well we do still have some cooking oil," holding up a small flask of milky yellow liquid.

"Yes! Exactly," said Duke, "a fire ship!"

Pazamor was a little lost. "What do you mean a fire ship Duke?"

"We have no time to waste – let us get on with the tasks in hand."

Pazamor started to stuff leaves and rocks under blankets near the fire to create the effect of them asleep in the camp.

Meanwhile Duke and Benedict grabbed more branches and continued to lash them together with stripped tree bark, completing a raft.

They piled as much burnable fuel, such as branches, dried grass and leaves as possible onto the raft and Benedict soaked it in the vegetable oil he had. He even found some plants that when squeezed produced similar oil to that he used for cooking.

"We have to time this just right. Get Paz, Ben."

The three of them waited under a full moon, an owl hooting in the starry night sky.

Soon a small rowing boat silently approached the shore. A crew of five motley men got out led by a man with one hand. Even in the little light from the moon they looked scary.

As they disappeared into the forest towards the abandoned camp, Pazamor, Benedict and Duke advanced towards their boat.

Benedict and Pazamor carried the raft and Duke walked up front. As they got closer to the boat it was evident that one man was still in it, but before he could raise the alarm Duke had taken his small crossbow and fired it, hitting the man directly in the heart. He slumped to the bottom of the boat, clutching the bolt in his hand.

Duke quickly climbed into the boat and pushed the body overboard, while Benedict and Pazamor placed the raft in the water and tied it to the rowing boat.

Benedict and Pazamor started rowing, while Duke attempted to get a light.

In the distance they could hear angry shouts.

"I guess they found us," smiled Pazamor.

"Keep rowing Paz!" whispered Benedict.

"Got it!" said Duke excitedly, having started a small fire.

Benedict quickly passed Duke a small candle.

"Thanks Ben," said Duke.

He lit the candle and put it to one side to assist with the rowing.

By now the pirate scouting party were on the beach angrily waving swords at them.

"Do you think they need a lift?" joked Pazamor.

"It's too crowded," smiled Duke.

"You better light that raft Ben, the current is going the wrong way to take the raft towards the ship," said Duke, as Benedict lit the raft by placing the candle inside it. "You head for Port Kepland and I will catch you up."

Benedict had placed the candle in a small alcove of the raft to avoid the wind catching it and blowing it out. This created a slow burning of the raft and gave more time for Duke to get as close as possible to the pirate ship before setting fire to it with the raft.

Duke jumped into the cold water, grabbed the small rope that had kept the raft tied to the boat and tugged it as he swam towards the large ship.

By now the fire was starting to really catch alight and he was not far from the pirate ship. However, the alarm was raised and the pirates knew what was happening. Duke grabbed some old fishing line he had in one of his very wet pockets and managing to secure this to a crossbow bolt tied the other end to the raft securely. With difficulty he managed to shoot the bolt at the ship and it lodged in the bottom just above the water line.

By now some of the pirate crew were trying to get buckets of water to hand to throw at the raft and put out the raft's fire. Duke shot off a volley of bolts hitting three of the crew, one falling in the water below, one dropping a bucket and the other pinned to a mast.

Quickly he started to swim for Port Kepland, narrowly avoiding the returned crossbow fire from the ship's crow nest.

The raft had lodged itself on the pirate ship from several crossbow bolts that Duke had secured around the edges beforehand and the fire had now spread to the ship.

Pazamor and Benedict reached Port Kepland without any trouble.

"Can you see Duke?" asked Benedict.

Pazamor looked intently into the darkness. "Yes, I can, he is west of the beach – let's go!"

After tying the boat to Port Keplands small dilapidated pier Pazamor and Benedict jumped onto the pebbled beach below and ran towards Duke as quickly and as close to him, without entering the cold water, as they could.

Benedict took a large silver symbol from a chain around his neck and turned it to reflect the moon's light.

Duke could make this out and headed towards it, even though he was getting tired by now. He swam towards it with his dying strength, the cold water zapping his life force.

As Duke reached the beach he was shivering, hypothermia was starting to set in.

Benedict took his cloak and wrapped it around Duke.

"Come on let's find somewhere warm!" he said.

The three of them headed towards the closest ale house they could find – 'The Black Swan'.

When they arrived inside Duke was still shivering from the cold. As they entered the eyes of the locals were upon the three of them, looking at them suspiciously. One of the locals left through a back door.

"You wouldn't be a pirate would you?" said the barman, eyeing up Duke.

"No I'd be a squire and it was me that set the pirate ship on fire!" said Duke, in a shivering voice.

"Is this true Brother?" the barman asked of Benedict, recognising him as a man of truth.

"Indeed it is, Duke is a fine warrior and deserves your respect. We need the use of your fire kind sir," said Benedict, pointing at the fire in the middle of the large room and Duke, whom was still shivering from the cold.

"Yes, of course, but you will still need to answer to our man at arms."

Benedict smiled as he and Pazamor took Duke to the fire and quickly undressed him, drying him with a blanket from a sack.

Benedict quickly set about boiling some water and took some herbs, placing these in the small pot.

Pazamor gave Duke a cloak he had spare and placed Dukes wet garments around the warm stones holding the fire.

The door opened and a small thin figure cloaked in dark blue entered, their face hidden from view.

The figure removed its hood to reveal – Sapphira!

"Hello," she said, "looks like I missed all the fun!" looking at Duke with a wicked smile.

She walked over to the group and greeted each with a hug.

She hugged Duke last of all and for a little longer than the rest of the group - he stopped shivering.

Benedict passed him the herbal tea he had made and he soon felt revived and refreshed.

The front door opened again and a man-at-arms appeared flanked by two other guards and the man they had seen walk out of the back door earlier, cowering behind them. The man at arms looked straight at Duke, "You are requested for questioning," pointing at Duke.

Benedict stood forward and pulled back his brown cloak revealing a large silver cross-like symbol hanging around his neck.

The man at arms looked closely at the middle of it.

"This is the Celthina Seal," said Benedict.

The guard bowed his head and knelt forward kissing it.

"I am in charge of these people and we are on Church business."

"Yes, of course Brother. You and your friends are welcome in Port Kepland.

"Perhaps you could assist us further, come and sit by the fire," said Benedict.

"Kent, brother, my name is Kent," said the man-at-arms.

"I am Benedict."

"Sapphira," she said bowing her head slightly.

"Pazamor," smiling.

"Duke," with eyes to the roof.

"So have you come about the mysterious disappearances and large earth mounds around the town?" asked Kent.

They all shared information about what they had learnt of the Kraytos Demon.

"Shall we all get some sleep and check out the town tomorrow?" asked Pazamor.

Sapphira laughed playfully, "We could, but we won't see any of these Kraytos Demons as they are creatures of the night!"

"The lady is right," said the man-at-arms, "we have noticed enhanced activity over the last few sunrises and particularly at night, as if they are looking for something."

"The hilt of the Sorcerer's Sword, no doubt!" suggested Duke.

"The most activity has been around the graveyards," mentioned Kent.

"Torrum told me to avoid these," said Sapphira.

"Well, know that we are together I think we should investigate," proposed Duke.

"Isn't it going to be a bit spooky doing this at night? questioned Pazamor.

"Sounds fun!" laughed Benedict.

"Well, I must go," said the man-at-arms."

"Wait ..." said Sapphira, "have you heard of someone called 'Jack the Rabbit'?"

"Oh yes! A colourful character is old Jack."

"Where can we find him?" asked Sapphira.

"Try over there by the corner of the room," said Kent. Pointing to an old man slumped at a table with six large empty tankards and a small shaggy dog by his feet.

The man-at-arms left the tavern.

Sapphira looked at Jack the Rabbit and then at Pazamor.

"Could you talk to him? He stinks too much for my liking!" she whispered.

"We'll wait here," laughed Benedict and Duke slapping Pazamor on the back, propelling him forward so fast that he slipped and flew into the table Jack was sat at.

"Whoops!" shouted Pazamor as the tankards crashed to the floor and he landed on the dog's tail.

"WOOF! WOOF! barked the small dog, waking the old man from his stupor.

"Who the heck are you?" said the man removing a tankard from his lap and grabbing Pazamor by the scruff of the neck.

"Umm… sorry – I am Pazamor and you must be Jack the Rabbit?"

The man let go of Pazamor and laughed loudly, "That I am mate. Not too hard to work out! Pointing to two dead rabbits around his neck.

"So what do you want?"

"Information, I guess," said Pazamor.

"Yes, but what information?" looking at Pazamor, as if he was the mad one.

Time and space shimmered around Jack.

"Well you got this far, good work son!   As for the hilt of the sword you seek, the final part of the puzzle, it can be found below the eastside of the graveyard. One of the crypts will lead the way and one of your group is better suited to the task than the others. Take care Young Pazamor."

Time and space once again shimmered around Jack.

"Well?" asked Jack.

"Thank you!" replied Pazamor.

Jack shrugged his shoulders and lay back on his seat, as if to sleep again.

Pazamor joined his group and explained what he had learnt.

"Let us go then," said Sapphira. "The graveyard is to the west of the town. I passed it on the way here."

Duke got changed back into his clothes, which were pretty dry by now and they were all refreshed enough to continue with their journey.

They left the tavern at the dead of night. It felt very eerie, not just under the moonlight but the quietness of the town itself. They walked along a cobbled path, passing shops and houses. Occasionally a dog would bark and a candle could be seen from a window, flickering in the distance, but generally the light of the moon lit their way.

As they started to leave the town their walk became more inclined, as if walking up a steady hill.

Soon they could see a church in front of them, its steeple standing out on the starry horizon.

A strange pungent, rotting smell permutated the graveyard, with a spooky mist shrouding it. The moonlight making the scene even scarier and more disconcerting.

"Well, who is going to take on this task?" asked Pazamor.

"I will," replied Benedict, "this is my territory," he said with a smile.

The four of them looked to the east side of the graveyard and carefully explored the graves for clues, especially the crypt type.

One crypt stood out from the rest, it had a metal fence surrounding it, but the gate was locked.

Pazamor, Sapphira, Duke and Benedict had completed their search of the other graves – this was the only one they had not been able to search properly.

They carefully examined the lock.

"We could do with Katrina's help here," said Duke, smiling at the rest of the group.

"Let me have a look," said Pazamor.

Sapphira watched quietly.

Pazamor took a small piece of wire from his sack, placed it into the lock and carefully turned it in an attempt to pick the lock. Snap!

"Whoops!" said Pazamor, "I think I've broken it!"

"Paz!" said Duke in a joking tone.

"Let me deal with the lock," spoke Sapphira in a quiet voice.

Pazamor moved aside.

Sapphira just stood in front of the lock for a moment quietly observing it and then took a small vile of liquid from her belt. She poured this chemical onto the lock's metal and a pungent gas arose from it. 'SNAP!' The lock was free – broken, it fell to the floor.

Duke pulled open the gate and it swung open with a large creaking sound, as if it had not been opened for many summers. The group entered.

Before them lay a tombstone which had a compass point on top of it, not unlike what they had seen before at Fort Nomad and Troll Tower.

Benedict and Sapphira examined the inscriptions very closely.

"This one means gas and this one death," said Sapphira pointing to two separate symbols.

"Yes," agreed Benedict, "the undead themselves could be protecting the last piece of the Sorcerer's Sword – the hilt. If you are happy with it I will take the tests and retrieve this item for us?"

Sapphira nodded, as did Duke and Pazamor in agreement.

"We aren't going to move this slab, it weighs a tone!" said Duke after trying to push it aside with his shoulder.

Benedict smiled and sounded a note from his throat that lifted the tomb's slab high into the air.

Duke, Pazamor and Sapphira copied the note. As they took over holding the object steady Benedict changed the tone and it moved aside. As they stopped sounding the note the slab fell to the ground breaking in two.

Peering into the tomb a set of stone steps could be seen extending below.

Pazamor passed the magic gemstone to Benedict, who thanked him and the rest of the group with a hug. They all wished Benedict luck as he disappeared down the steps into the darkness below.

*

As the rest of the group was wondering what to do a crumpling noise was heard behind them.

"What was that?" whispered Pazamor.

Sapphira froze, "That is the Kraytos Demon!"

"How many of them?" asked Duke as he swiftly took out his crossbow and lent against the crypt for cover.

"I sense three, no six - maybe more – they are moving too fast for me. They are being drawn to us for some reason."

"We must get off the ground. It's not safe!" said Duke.

"The crypt over there," motioned Pazamor.

The three of them ran to it leaping on top of grave stones as fast as they could to get to it. The ground moved under their feet, as if a small earthquake was under them.

Just as they reached the safety of the stone tomb two Kraytos Demons pounded out of the earth. Their long ears covered their faces but quickly lifted up to reveal a large, round, blotted face with sharp teeth and a ghastly scream that curdled the blood.

Duke wasted no time in saying hello and fired off a volley of three bolts from his small crossbow straight into one of the demons heads.   One of the bolts hit an eye, green liquid came oozing out and exploded all around them.   The monster let out a scream and held its eye with one hand.

The other demon was now out of the ground and leapt in front of Pazamor, who was stood frozen in shock and fear.

Sapphira quickly took two small micro flasks containing the liquid vinegar and threw them together at the demon facing Pazamor. This demon also screamed as the vinegar dripped down its thick skin, burning it and giving off gasses through its bubbling skin, where the vinegar had made contact.

Duke took his short sword and quickly thrust it through the same demons chest.

The demon fell to the floor it body jumping up and down and green liquid oozing from the large wound created.

As Duke retrieved his sword it fell into pieces, the creatures own acid having dissolved it.

"Quickly we must leave this place."

A miner bird hovered in the air screaming, "Intruders! Intruders!" as it headed north towards Dragon Teeth Mountain.

"Kraytos is near!" announced Sapphira, "that is his miner bird – I would recognise that cursed voice anywhere."

"Never mind that now," said Duke we have to deal with his demons for the moment and we must have better weapons, throwing the remains of his short sword to the floor.

The group jumped from tomb to tomb stone and avoided the floor of the graveyard as best they could in a bid to avoid detection from the demons below.

"The church!" pronounced Pazamor, "Let's head for the Church."

No one stood to argue – it was the best idea in the light that they had no other ideas at this moment in time and time was not on their side.

They reached the main door and jumped to the alcove which had a stone floor. Sapphira tested the door – it was unlocked. As she swung it open it creaked heavily and revealed a dimly lit hallway. Behind them two more Kraytos Demons were coming out of the ground just in front of the door they had entered. Duke quickly slammed the door shut and pushed a large block of wood across the door – effectively locking it from the inside.

"It will not hold them back long," he said.

"I don't suppose there is any vinegar stored here?"

"Well I have tried their wine and if you ask me it tastes like it!" joked Duke.

Duke looked at his bow – "I only have two shots left, not enough to take two of these monsters down."

"What do you have Pazamor?"

"A small knife," pulling a pocket knife from his sack.

"Sapphira?" asked Duke, in hope of a better weapon.

"Sorry, just my spells mainly, and I am unsure which to use on them."

"A pity you can't change water into vinegar," joked Pazamor, as steam started to appear from the main door. The wood started to burn from the creature's acid as they tried to break down the door.

"That's it!" said Sapphira. "I can change water into wine, which although not enough on its own is with another spell I have that will change the wine into VINEGAR!"

"Give me all the water you have and protect me while I make the spells."

"Help me Paz," said Duke as he grabbed a pew and set it against the door as a barricade. Pazamor understood and did the same with another pew, after about the third pew the door, or what was left of it fell off its hinges and disintegrated to the floor.

The pews temporarily filled the gap and infuriated the Kraytos Demons as they lashed at these with all their strength, smashing them into small bits in a bid to get to their quarry.

Sapphira was over by the church's stone font and having further filled it with all their water supplies had just completed the first spell successfully and turned this into wine.

"Smells nice," said Duke, "better than these things," referring to the Kraytos Demons.

Pazamor was busily pushing a fourth pew into the fresh gap created from the others that had been destroyed. As he did so Duke let of a last volley of two bolts at the closest demon's face. It screamed in agony and knocked the other demon beside it over as it swayed from side to side in pain.

Sapphira had just conjured Haddon again and it was him that would provide the last bit of the spell. She held out her hand to him and he smelt the tiniest drop of vinegar on it and then ran in circles around the font until he disappeared in a blaze of light.

Pazamor stared – although he could not see Haddon he could see a bright light surrounding the font as Sapphira was casting her spell with words of power.

Just as one of the demons had fallen to the floor another two came through the door pushing aside their dying colleague and heading towards Pazamor and Duke, whom were already beating a hasty retreat to the font, where Sapphira was stood.

"This had better work," shouted Duke as he and Pazamor ducked from a flying piece of pew.

Three of the demons were now fast approaching the group.

"Actomos!" shouted Sapphira lifting her hands above her head. Suddenly the water in the font flew up in the air carried by a whirlwind created by Haddon. "Vantamos!" she further said, pointing her fingers at the advancing demons. Haddon sprayed the liquid at the advancing demons with all his force. As it hit them they dissolved into a pool of green liquid slime before the group.

Both Pazamor and Duke stared at each other until Duke broke the silence, "That was a pretty good trick," he said.

"Enough to give us some breathing space," said Sapphira.

As they were recovering their energy a little old man dressed in black appeared behind them.

"What is all this commotion in the house of the Universal Spirit?" he asked.

"We have been fighting Kraytos Demons!" announced Pazamor.

"Ye, been fighting! Fighting in my house!" said the old man.

"Well, just a little tussle," announced Duke, while hugging a bleeding arm, caused from a shrapnel of wood from the broken pews."

"My pews!" He exclaimed, but before he could say anything further Sapphira grabbed his attention and mesmerised him with an enchantment spell. He was now under her command.

"So," she said, "How can we get to Dronagon's Castle?"

"Apart from boat there is only one other way - a secret passage from this very Church, it was built by the first King at the same time the castle was built – only a handful of people know of its existence."

"Show us this secret passage!" instructed Sapphira.

"You are looking at it. The passage is under the font in front of you."

Duke wasted no time and began to push the font with all his strength. Pazamor assisted but it did not budge being made of solid heavy stone.

"How do we open it?" asked Sapphira.

The priest pointed above the font revealing a massive chain system which held the font lid.

Pazamor inspected the system closely and quickly had the answer. He found a turning wheel on the wall, hidden by a curtain. By turning this he was able to lower the font's lid.

"Give me a hand Duke," he said as he locked the lid onto the font with four clasps from the lid. I will need some help in pushing it aside, I think."

Pazamor turned the wheel on the wall again, this time in the opposite direction making the chain pull upwards and it become taught as it took the bigger strain of the entire font, lifting it from the ground.

Sapphira and Duke looked on. "It's a long way down," said Duke looking below.

"Well at least there are steps!" pointed out Pazamor, having locked the chain mechanism, the font suspended high above them.

"What are we waiting for? Asked Duke, "let's rescue the King."

Chapter 14
Lord Kraytos

Hidden away in the depths of the castle's dungeons lay King Dronagon on a bed of rotting hay. The accommodation was a far cry from what he was normally used to and the smell down here stank of death and disease!

The King could not see too much as only a couple of lanterns lit the entire dungeon floor. The floor itself was cold, damp and filthy with excrement from past tenants. Red stains suggested blood and yellow urine amongst the rotting flesh of rats either killed by the dungeon keeper or past inmates.

King Dronagon himself was a proud man, although a little large, having lived on the indulgences provided with his title – too much food and not enough exercise!

He had shoulder length blond hair though with a beard and moustache that was brown in colour.

In the distance he could hear some keys turning in a lock, a door slamming and footsteps approaching.

"You!" he sounded in surprise. "What do you think you are doing? Let me go this instance!" shouted the King.

"Let you go?" taunted the man before him, "Never! You are my slave now, as is your kingdom mine."

"Lord Kraytos I will give you money and power, just let me go from here."

"LORD! LORD Kraytos ..." he laughed. "My title is King Kraytos now and you bow to me. I have been your wizard for over ten summers and in all that time you did not afford me any new title save the one I already had. Well Dronagon I do not wait forever – I take what I want. You are the one that can wait now – until your death!"

Kraytos turned his back and began to walk down the passage he had descended.

"Give me back my Kingdom. Give me back my birth rite!" shouted King Dronagon after him.

"It is mine now! All mine!" shouted Kraytos after the King as he left the dungeon slamming the door behind him.

A lantern went out leaving only one all on its own and even more darkness and despair in its wake.

Kraytos retired to his tower, which was known as Dagmar's Tower. From this he could see the entire lands of Dronagon's Kingdom below. However, he had plans to change this, soon it would be known as Kryatos's Domain and he would be in charge.

Kraytos himself was a tall thin man, a typical wizard stereotype, except he wasn't that old in the physical or at least he thought this at around the age of fifty summers, although his soul was much older. He had long, black hair, which had still not aged and dark green eyes, from a failed chemical experiment involving argon gas, large bushy eyebrows and a long pointed nose. He had once been a good person but had been turned by selfishness and seeking power at all costs for himself, rather than sharing it with others.

As he sat in his wizard's study his miner bird came crashing through the top tower's open window squawking out its latest message: 'Intruders! Intruders!' it squawked.

Kraytos was intrigued, who would stand up to him as a high wizard of the black arts? He took a crystal ball from one of his many library shelves and stared deeply into it. He sprinkled a little water on the ball to remove a bit of dust which enabled him to see better what was going on.

After turning it in his hands a little it began to glow slightly and within he could see Sapphira, Pazamor and Duke fighting the Kraytos Demons in the Cemetery and beating them.

"Torrum!" He exclaimed after spying one of his apprentices – namely Sapphira.

"What is that bumbling old fool up to. I thought my soldiers would have killed her and him by now – and who are your friends?" said Kraytos talking to himself and spying Duke and Pazamor more intently. "Never mind you will all die!" he claimed in defiance. "My grand weapon is nearly ready now and nothing will stop it – not even the great wizard Torrum!" shaking his fist in the air. "Tanous!" he shouted.

A tall guard dressed in full black battle armour appeared. "You called Sir?"

"Double the watch and call out the black guards – we have uninvited guests on the way to see us."

Tanous clicked his feet together, banged his chest with his fist and left to increase the castle guard.

Kraytos looked out of the tower window to the kingdom below.

"Where is my apprentice? Odil! Odil where are you?"

"Here Master, in your study."

"But you are not in the physical!"

No Master, I am not - I am in the astral, moving through the shadows and darkness of your room.

"You spend too much of your time in this dream world Odil! Did you see into my crystal the enemies I would seek to destroy?"

"Yes Master – I did."

"Then go and find these cursed people and destroy them!" he laughed menacingly.

"Of course Master!"

There was a flash of golden light and Odil was gone from the tower and flying through the night air looking for his prey.

Kraytos moved over to a part of his latest toy – a massive silver concave mirror based at the highest point of Dagmar's Tower. He marvelled at his work and pulled a small lever to test it. A low frequency noise could be heard emanating from the dish. He quickly went to his work desk and examined the small mirrored tetrahedron (like a pyramid but with a triangular base – an object with only four triangular sides of the same size and shape) the size of a fist. He had been working on this for over a season and marvelled at its complexity as he picked it up and turned it in his hand. It too emitted a small noise in tune with the large concave mirror. Kraytos laughed to himself – "I have done it – at last! – Ha! Ha! Ha! Ha!"

He grabbed the small tetrahedron and took it down to the next level for his chief alchemist to examine.

"I want 10,000 of these units as soon as possible. We will sell them to the rich at first and then when we have more money from them we will give them to the poor for free! Everyone will have my new toy – and then my toy will have them! Soon I will have an army bigger than any before us and we will crush that cursed troll nation and eradicate them from this Domain and all Domains forever."

He looked at the alchemist, as if knowing what he was thinking.

"Use the stupid king's money! Have his gold melted down and sell it to finance this project."

"What of the soldiers and your loyal workers, they will need paying too Lord Kraytos?"

"Of course they will but soon they will work for me for free - as their King and Master," he cackled with a psychotic laugh that emanated throughout the castle walls and beyond...

Kraytos returned to his study. Although he could live anywhere in the castle, as it was now under his control, he still preferred Dagmar's Tower. A tower was the true place for any wizard or Master – away from people its solitude provided peace to work one pointedly without any unwanted interferences.

He went to sit on his seat of power, a large throne-like seat made of dark marble, with several large white quartz crystals laid in the arms and head of the chair. As he sat and meditated on how he would take over the people of this world and how the trolls would pay for killing the one true love of his life so many summers before – those of the black lodge took over his brain. He saw wars, killing, buildings and lands on fire at the centre of this was him holding up a small silver pyramid shape triumphantly.

*

The group continued down the wooden spiral staircase until they reached the bottom of a large cave alcove. Sapphira said some words of power and Haddon glowed like a small ball of light more than lighting their way ahead through the dark caverns.

Pazamor took out his father's compass – "We travel north," he said, "this is good."

"Indeed," said Duke.

"How long is it before your enchantment spell will wear off the priest?" asked Duke of Sapphira.

"It lasts no longer than a day unless I send a 'familiar' or 'wraith' to keep those enchanted for the duration I keep the familiar or wrath in my control. Those enchanted under its instructions can be held thus for a greater or lesser time, dependant on that control. This is how Kraytos has stolen several of the king's guards for his own purposes. Others have been bought or killed off, if not in line with his thinking."

They continued north along the cave's corridors until they noticed a levelling off and slight dripping of water. Cracks could be seen in the ceiling above and it was from here the cold salt water dripped, the sound echoing through the caves many passages and creating a winter look with the white crusted ceiling and slippery floor.

"We must be passing under the sea, Dragon Teeth Mountain cannot be far away now," said Duke.

"Yes," agreed Sapphira pointing at the cracks in the ceiling from which the water was dripping.

"We wouldn't want the walls or ceiling to collapse," voiced Pazamor. The others had thought it but not spoken of it.

"Shhhh!" said Sapphira, "Do not use your power of speech to bring about something none of us would want."

"I was only joking," said Pazamor.

"This is not the time or place Pazamor," said Sapphira sternly, "Lord Kraytos already knows we are on our way to him – he will be prepared – so must we!"

"What of Benedict?" asked Pazamor.

Sapphira paused for a moment extending her aura and sending out a telepathic contact to Benedict.

She opened her eyes and continued walking again with Pazamor and Duke following.

"Benedict is still fine, a little out of breath, but still fine. He has not yet found the Sorcerer's Sword hilt but continues to search. I have shown him this secret passage in his mind's eye and he will follow us as soon as he can," said Sapphira.

"I could really do with that weapon!" answered Duke.

Sapphira laughed, "You have other weapons at your disposal Duke. You should not simply relay on physical weapons for your defence or attack.   The best form of defence is using the force of the attacker against themselves. That way it is their Karma and not yours that is at fault."

"All the same Sapphira those skills you mention are untested and yet my sword hand and archery eye are utilised as polished skills," replied Duke.

"I think the answer is somewhere in-between," laughed Pazamor. "I would be willing to try my magic but if it failed I would prefer to have my brain and intelligence available as a back up!"

"We have all had it then, there is no hope for any of us," joked Duke.

[The group made good progress, so much so that soon they found themselves under the centre of Dragon Teeth Mountain.]

"It is very warm here," noted Pazamor.

"There is probably an active volcano underneath us," voiced Sapphira.

"A what?" asked Pazamor.

"Do you read anything?" questioned Sapphira with a smile.

The question reminded Pazamor of his little book. "Yes, of course I do but often I have to borrow books as they are so prohibitively expensive."

"I am sorry," said Sapphira, "I did not mean it in that way. I am lucky enough to have lots of books from my Master's library and you are welcome to share them some time."

"Thanks!" replied Pazamor, "I may well take you up on that offer."

The group stopped at the bottom of a large winding stone staircase cut into a giant stalagmite or stalactite, it was difficult to differentiate which type it was as it was joined at the middle.

"We should rest here," remarked Duke.

The group settled down to rest and eat some provisions before the great climb ahead of them.

Pazamor sat down on the step to read his book while Sapphira and Duke discussed a plan of rescue:

'On seeking the Universal Spirit...

Although signs can be found of an outward nature, they are only of a temporary happiness; it is within your own heart that you will find everlasting peace. Though there are many churches and other such buildings built to worship me, do not forget that your body is also one such temple and that when you sit down quietly to meditate or pray you can find me deep within you.

"It is good to grow up in a church, but not die in one."

Do not allow others to tell you what I am rather find out for yourself. You must ask the question deeply – 'WHO AM I?'

The group started to pack away their things, having rested sufficiently and gained further energy from this. They had all eaten some nourishing coco provisions that Benedict had prepared for them a day earlier from a plant found in the troll's forest.

All of a sudden Pazamor froze. 'Crackle! Crackle!' he heard. He looked to a corner of the room from where he had heard the noise, but although he could see nothing he knew something was there watching them, while they packed away their items.

"Something is wrong!" remarked Sapphira.

"Yes, I feel it too," some being is watching us.

Duke looked carefully around before saying "Whoooo!" and whispering perhaps it is a ghost!"

Pazamor spoke, "No Duke this entity is strong I have heard and felt similar experiences when meditating and latter the Master has explained it was him watching over my progress from a distance. I hear things that are beyond this physical world."

"I am afraid I would have to agree," said Sapphira, while I cannot hear anything there is a dim light in that corner, suggesting some kind of life force. I think it is ...

"AHHHH! She let out a scream as the force had sped to her, surrounding Sapphira's head."

"It is attacking her," said Pazamor.

"I can see that!" said Duke, "but how can I fight what I cannot see?" Holding a knife in his hand.

Haddon disappeared in a puff of smoke as Sapphira lost control of him and it all went dark around them.

"Rats!" said Duke as he hurriedly tried to find his tinder box and light a fire to see again.

Pazamor however could perceive a bit more than Duke, making out a red hazy aura around Sapphira's head as she struggled on the floor.

Pazamor concentrated hard on his ajna chakra and thought 'TANG! Help us Tang!'

There was a massive flash of white light that came from Pazamor's Crown Chakra and he found himself out of his body as it fell to the ground and in front of him was Odil surprised to see him with his hands squeezing Sapphira's head.

Pazamor wasted no time in using the element of surprise and knocked Odil flying, with a big push of his arms, Odil actually being of a smaller build than Pazamor.

Odil hit the floor with a thud. All around had a golden glow to it but Pazamor noted a silvery rope like cord that protruded from Odil's Stomach and a similar such cord from his own head to his body which lay lifeless on the floor.

He noted that Duke was looking over his and Sapphira's body and that Sapphira was trying to recover from the astral attack.

Odil was now on his feet and facing Pazamor in a standoff – as if to assess this new enemy threat.

Suddenly Sapphira appeared before Pazamor in golden astral form and between him and Odil.

Now Odil was very scared and tried to escape but before he could Sapphira grabbed hold of his astral cord. There was a massive flash of white light again and Pazamor awoke back into the darkness he left, after seeing Odil disappearing at lightning speed, being recalled to his body – Sapphira's astral body in tow.

"I am ok now Duke," said Pazamor as he regained consciousness.

"Do you have any candles left?" asked Duke.

"Yes, one that Ben gave me. I will try and get it from my pack."

"How is Sapphira Paz – I heard you leave this plane in your astral body – pretty impressive! I thought you could only do that from sleep."

"I think I had some help! Sapphira has gone after the entity to give him some of his own medicine."

"Click! Click! Click"

Pazamor could hear Duke attempting to get a light from his tinder box within the darkness, scraping his knife against a special stone.

"Have you found that candle yet? Quizzed Duke again.

Pazamor struggled a little more and then managed to locate it at the bottom of his pack.

"Snap!"

"Whoops!" said Pazamor, "Sorry Duke I think you have two candles now," handing Duke to parts of a broken candle in the darkness.

"Hughh," sighed Duke trying to find the best bit in the darkness. "Here Paz, hold it near the sparks – I have the tinder there."

As Odil was flung back into his body Sapphira let go at the last possible minute; holding her concentration to keep her in this parallel astral world of life and avoiding her own astral form being flung back to its own body.

She looked around within her new settings and immediately recognised it to be Dagmar's Tower. She must be on the middle level, she thought. Looking out of the window she could see more guards than normal on the battlements and few weaknesses in their defence.

Odil tried to wake up in the physical world.

'Oh no you don't – you snake!' thought Sapphira as she put one astral hand through his head and the other in his solar plexus – moving both in a slow stirring motion.

Odil physically vomited in his bed.

Though Sapphira could have snapped his life force she merely stretched it to the point of breaking but then stopped.

'That will put you out of action for a while', she thought.

She left Odil on the bed in a cataleptic coma state, knowing it would take him a couple of sunrises to fully recover – hopefully giving the group enough time to complete their mission, without any more interference from him.

While Odil was out of action she flew up through the building passing through the building floor in the same way a ghost might walk through a wall, until she reached the top most section.

Alighting the pinnacle point of the tower she found Kraytos working away on the large concave dish.

It was strange that he was so interested in it – after all they were only reflectors – just like the one in the Celthina Monastery – two on their own would not be enough to do anything – to do anything properly you would need three.

Then it dawned on Sapphira the Kraytos Demon was no more than a diversion to hide what Kraytos was really up to.

She flew through the tower a bit more and discovered the chief alchemist with some ten others and a wizard utilising a duplication spell. Between them they were filling the room with hundreds, perhaps thousands of small silver-like pyramidal type objects.

One took a box of these outside – she followed to see him putting it onto a horse and cart with others like it. The cart left bound for Wizards Way – or at least that is what it sounded like.

Sapphira was about to leave when she noticed that several hundred soldiers were building a massive stone structure within the Castle Walls. Although unfinished it resembled an equilateral triangle, in shape. The soldiers looked like they had been enslaved by Kraytos through an enchantment spell in order to build this and a tent holding a wraith nearby, confirmed her suspicions.

Suddenly Sapphira awoke in her physical body. "AHH! She screamed, holding her head in her hands.

She had a massive headache and it throbbed like mad. I wish Benedict was here she said.

Just then Duke managed to light the tinder and the candles Pazamor had given him.

Before them stood Benedict.

Duke laughed, "Well, by the Gods – you have made it!" referring to what he had hanging from a rope around his waist.

"Indeed I have my friend," replied Benedict unhooking and tossing the Sorcerer's Sword Hilt to Duke, whom quickly grabbed it before it could hit the floor.

As Duke attempted to assemble the sword Benedict walked over to Sapphira and gently touched her head with both hands. Closing his eyes, standing still and lifting his head up to the ceiling, he quietly meditated. As he did so Sapphira began to relax more until she began to close her eyes. Benedict laid her down from her sitting position onto the floor and she began to sleep quietly.

"The healing will take a while, we will need to wait until then before moving on," he whispered.

"So what happened then Ben?" asked Pazamor in a quiet voice.

"Yes, come on tell us the full story," said Duke as he managed to slot the sword blade and handle together.

"Well ok then," answered Benedict as he sat down with Pazamor and Duke around the candle light:

"After shortly leaving you and making my way down the catacombs I came across something protruding from the earth – it looked white in colour despite only having a dim red light to see from the stone Pazamor had given me." Benedict handed the red gemstone to Duke, whom turned it over in his hand, admiring its beauty, while working out where to place it within the Sorcerer's Sword.

Benedict continued the story, "Yes, you guessed it! It was the remains of some skeleton from some poor soul and an intersecting tunnel was in front of this. One that was fresh and not part of the original design. I knew that the Kraytos Demons had been at work and even discovered the lair which led to the Sorcerers Hilt. I knew that I would have to act fast if we were to get there first. I needn't have worried though as it was well protected.

What I did notice was that the Demons had been eating whatever flesh was left from the dead. They seem to enjoy this more than that of the living – though they can quickly turn the living to the dead! I continued down the central passage more prepared for a fight than anything else but what met my eyes was a little disturbing. The small corridor, along which I had been travelling opened up into a large room with a high ceiling above, which was full of hundreds of small holes near the highest ceiling point. On the floor was a green mass of gunk that smelt awful, similar to that we have seen near the holes the Kraytos Demons emerge from. In the middle of the room were five tomb caskets - all closed. I summarised that one would hold the reward and the others certain death. Those demons that had entered this room had somehow met an untimely death – how? I did not know but had to quickly work it out unless I was to follow suit. I could hear something approaching from behind and towards me. I looked for somewhere to hide. Using my cloak I was able to fit myself in a tight muddy alcove and disguise myself with earth and some dead bones left hanging there. It was risky but I hoped my plan would work – I tossed the gemstone into the open space and held my breath, meditating I put my body to sleep and stepped outside of it in my astral form, my physical body hidden from view as if it wasn't there.

Sure enough the monster approached and ran right past me and must have seen the gemstone as it headed straight for it. As the demon picked it up and began to admire it in his hands hundreds of small bats came down from the ceiling and plunged their teeth into his flesh, quickly tearing him apart. Within a blink of an *eye* there was nothing left – although the creature had managed to kill some of the killer bats, those left alive ate their dead comrades. While I was still in the astral world I ventured forth and was able to pass through the walls of the coffins and see what lay in each one. It was the middle one which had steps that passed on further. With this in mind I re-entered my body and through the power of sound was able to lift the coffin lid while running, grabbing the gemstone and after entering the empty coffin quickly stopped the note I was sounding in order to let the lid drop shut again. Just before the bats could realise what was going on, being confused by the noise.

After travelling what felt like northwards in direction and downwards for an eternity things started to get warmer, until I reached a point where molten larva itself ran across my path, like a wide stream divides two pieces of land. Across from this I could clearly see the Sorcerer's Sword hilt, set in a small alcove in the middle of the cave wall – but out of reach!

I meditated for a moment on what to do, then I had the answer – I would walk through the river of molten larva and pick up the hilt. I tried to recall the technique my Master, Abbott Tarock, had shown me to overcome heat, as I hadn't done it for some time.

Throwing my hand in the air I shouted 'I am powerful!' At the top of my voice several times. Then I faced the molten larva and talked to it. I told it that I would pass through it and it would not harm me; that it would be like warm water and walking through rapids. When I could hear and feel my energy field buzzing around me I faced the larva stream. For a moment I just stared across it to the hilt – my goal!

Then I just stepped out into the larva and kept walking until I got to the other side. The heat was immense around me.

Looking down to my feet I was half expecting to see just bones but apart from losing some of the hair from my legs they were fine. It had felt as if I had simply walked across a very, very warm, red river with rapids.

I had made it! Retrieving the hilt I entered a tunnel to the left and opening a secret heavy, one way door [pointing to a cave wall that concealed an entrance]. I walked upwards to find you here."

"Wow!" said Pazamor, "you walked across burning, molten lava?"

"By the grace of the Universal Spirit and a respect for all life I believe we can do anything Pazamor," replied Benedict.

"I can't get the gemstone to fit the sword," mentioned Duke, fiddling with it further, while listening to Benedict.

"No," said Benedict, "it will take a Master to activate it properly."

Duke sighed, "Oh, well at least I have a decent sword now," swinging it through the air and admiring the craftsmanship of the blade and handle.

Chapter 15
Castle Dronagon

"Pazamor can you stay with Sapphira while I and Duke scout on ahead? It could be half a day before she recovers her full energy." said Benedict.

"Well ok, I guess I get to rest, read some more of my book and meditate a bit," said Pazamor smiling.

Benedict and Duke continued up the many stone stairs which lead to the castle. The sorcerer's stone helped light the way ahead. The cave walls glowed in a dim red with the light from the stone.

Eventually they reached the top, only to find their exit blocked by a large barred grill. Duke pushed on it, in a bid to try and release the grill but had no luck – it held fast.

In the corner of his eye he could see a heavy padlock that held the grill shut tight.

"Oh no!" said Duke, "I don't want to go all the way back down to get Paz!"

Benedict giggled, "There is no need for that," said Benedict, closing his eyes and sitting quietly on the stairs underneath the bars. "He will come to us."

Sure enough within a very short space of time Pazamor appeared, "Was it you calling me? Or you?" He asked, looking at Benedict and then Duke in turn.

"Which do you think?" replied Benedict looking Pazamor in the eye.

"I think it was you Ben, as I saw the symbol of the cross in my mind's eye but felt my solar plexus moving like mad."

"Indeed it was me Paz. Now can we get to the point and will you open this lock?"

Pazamor looked at it carefully –"It is easier than the last one," he ventured. Taking forth a small bent darning needle from his sack he tried to gently twist it in the lock. As he did so he could feel the small pins moving – "Just one to go!" he said.

He took another such needle, but this one was straight and inserted this in the lock also. A bit more twisting and he successfully managed to open the lock with a loud clicking sound.

"Well done Paz," said Duke, gently patting Pazamor on the back.

"Who is there?" asked a weak, but well refined voice in the semi-darkness.

Benedict quietly opened the grill and carefully made his way to the wall of the room and then towards where he had heard the voice. He could feel slime under his feet and the stink of rotting flesh. Something scurried past his foot – 'probably a rat' he thought.

Pazamor noticed the gemstone around Duke's neck and the Sorcerer's Sword in his belt – "Can I have that?" he whispered.

Duke passed Pazamor the items in question.

Within a moment of Pazamor having the Sword and gemstone he managed to successfully put the two together. The gemstone fitted the sword's hilt perfectly.

"How did you do that?" asked Duke.

"I don't know," replied Pazamor, "I just fiddled with it and it fitted."

With the gemstone now attached to the sword it now changed colour and instead of red it glowed blue. The light was enough to make out more of their surroundings but not enough to move as quickly as they would have liked.

Pazamor grabbed the sword by the hilt and used it as if it were a torch to light their way.

After a short while they could all see enough of the room, which they could recognise as a dungeon.

"Over here," spoke the soft voice again.

"My Lord," said Benedict bowing before someone that was obviously of high stature.

"We have come to rescue you Sire," spoke Duke, with Pazamor beside him, trying to shake off the mess from his feet.

"The keys for the cells are across from you on the wall opposite," pointed the King.

Pazamor handed the sword to Duke and then returned with the jailer keys. He unlocked the King's cell and Duke entered. With one well aimed swoop of the sword Duke smashed the manacles holding the King's feet together, freeing him.

The king was overwhelmed with gratitude. "Thank you!" he said, hugging each one of them and shaking their hands.

"Pazamor will you take the King to Sapphira for the moment? She will hopefully be well enough to guide him to safety. Too many of his guards are un-loyal here," whispered Duke.

"Wait!" said the King, "take this," handing Duke a valuable looking necklace from around his neck.

"The King's seal!" replied Benedict taking it from Duke and turning it over in his hand to carefully examine the large golden symbol on the end of the chain necklace, that looked very much like a coin, before putting it around his own neck.

"That is correct and those that are still loyal to me will recognise it as such. Take good care, and once again thank you for rescuing me," he said, as Pazamor showed him down the stone steps and explained where he would find Sapphira.

"I have a plan," said Duke. "Can you ask Sapphira to take the King to the safety of Port Kepland and create a diversion for us at the castle gate?" Ben.

"Give me a minute," said Benedict, sitting down to concentrate on sending the message telepathically to Sapphira. "It is done," he said, "Sapphira is feeling better, except for a headache, which does not help with spell casting, but fine to walk and can still create a mean concoction of alchemy, if needed."

As Benedict was saying this Duke went to the grill and re-locked its padlock, securing it once again. "We will need the keys Pazamor," whispered Duke.

"Ok let's go, follow my lead," said Duke, making his way to the main dungeon door.

"I hope one of these keys fits this big door," looking at the heavy wooden door that was reinforced with metal and rivets.

"Well try it and see young Paz," said Duke smiling.

Pazamor took the heavy keys and carefully looked at them, finding the largest key he tried the lock. Sure enough it worked and when he turned the lock it opened with a loud clang.

Duke acted quickly and raced through the door with lightening speed. Seeing a guard sat on the floor against the wall and now stirring from the noise of the door opening he quickly took the Sorcerer's Sword and hit the guard across the head with the handle of it, putting him back into the land of sleep again.

"Give me a hand Paz," said Duke as he grabbed the fallen guard, dragging him into the dungeon and locking him in the cell King Dronagon had resided in.

Duke took off his own cloths and changed into the uniform of the Black Guard they had just captured.

"A perfect fit!" he proclaimed.

"Well..." said Benedict.

"Oh, yes, the plan," said Duke, smiling again. "It is rather simple – to get as many guards as we can locked into this dungeon."

Benedict laughed, "Well I am sure we can assist," he said, taking out his staff and extending it to its full size, with a bashing motion and a comical expression on his face.

They scouted around the lower levels utilising the set of keys they had to open any doors they could find. Duke found a small armoury from a guard room, which he easily gained access because of his dress and looking about he discovered some bolts that fitted his crossbow perfectly, as well as a short sword for Pazamor.

Duke took some chains he also found from the store and wrapped them loosely around Pazamor's hands behind his back.

"What is that for?" asked Pazamor in surprise.

"I am pretending that you are a prisoner and Benedict is here to read you your last rites before we hang you." whispered Duke.

"Heck! If you are my friend who needs enemies!" replied Pazamor with eyes open wide in jest.

The group slowly advanced up through the levels of the castle.

In the second guard room the group was challenged by the Constable, who was head of castle security.

"What do you want in here? All should be on duty by command of King Kraytos," he said in a rough voice.

"We are to visit our Lord with a spy captured in the inner ward Sir," replied Duke, pushing Pazamor to the floor.

"Well take him to Dagmar's Tower for King Kraytos or Tanous but not the Keep – you halfwit. You know he prefers that place to here," pointing across the room to a small hole in the wall which served as a window, looking out onto Dagmar's Tower

"Yes, Sir of course Sir," said Duke hitting his chest and clicking his feet together, in a salute common to the Black Guard.

As they went higher they found the lobby area and from here the entrance door on the first floor of the building. Two guards were in it but this did not matter as they were exiting the building and not entering it. They nodded to each other as they passed.

As the group stood outside the Keep's entrance at the top of the steps the daylight hit them and they realised a new day was dawning. The sky was red in colour as the sun rose, blinding those that dared to look directly at it.

They walked down the stone steps and looked before them in amazement. In the inner Keep was what looked like a gigantic stone pyramid – though it was still incomplete.

Many soldiers and people were dragging large stones into the inner castle grounds with the support of rough masons who cut them into blocks. These were in turn overseen by freemasons, ensuring the more accurate cuts were made and tidying up any rough edges. The finished pieces of stone were slotted together like a giant puzzle.

Benedict watched as some pirates handed over slaves for money to work on Kraytos's master project. But what was the villain up to?

When they eventually reached Dagmar's Tower they stood outside the large solid silver double doors. Duke knocked hard on it. Some movement could be heard behind them and someone asked from behind what they wanted.

Duke responded, "We have a spy that needs interrogating by Tanous. The Constable told us to bring him here."

"Just a minute," said a voice from behind the door, "I am busy!"

The doors did not open in the normal way but rather slid across in a fashion neither of the group had seen before. Stood before them was a man dressed in colourful robes and holding a silver tetrahedron structure in one hand and some kind of potion within a glass vial in the other. "This is the last batch!" said the man excitedly, "hurry up and get in I need to finish my work."

The three of them entered, but before the man could call Tanous, Benedict whacked him hard over the head with his staff in one and took the flask with the other.

Duke grabbed the man before he could hit the ground. The tetrahedron continued to fall but Pazamor managed to catch it between his feet, as his hands were still tied behind his back.

"It looks like the same substance as the Kraytos Demons blood," said Benedict holding up the potion to the light.

"Well this object is no ordinary object it has vibration," said Pazamor awkwardly moving the object with his feet to Benedict.

"Wow!" said Duke looking into the room he was dragging the unconscious alchemist to. It was full of shelves stacked high with similar objects to what Benedict now held in his hand.

"What on earth is going on here?" asked Benedict aloud to himself.

"I might well ask the same question?" replied a gruff voice from behind – it was Tanous.

Duke quickly drew the Sorcerer's Sword and it gleamed blue as it was drawn from his holster. Benedict also produced his staff in a defensive posture, while Pazamor tried to release the chains Duke had placed on him.

Tanous laughed mockingly, "What is this? Just three of you to defeat an army?" slowly drawing a large double handed sword to defend himself.

He and Duke clashed swords while Benedict stood in front of Pazamor, as if to protect him.

Tanous clumsily swung the large two handed sword, due to the shortage of space, missing Duke narrowly as he ducked and instead hitting several of the pyramid type objects – smashing them onto the floor. One of them leaked a green liquid from its broken tip, similar to that they had seen in the flask.

Duke returned the favour with a thrust of the shorter Sorcerer's Sword but Tanous jumped back avoiding it and then lifting his own sword above his head brought it down towards Duke's head. Pazamor pushed Duke out of the way as it came crashing down onto the floor, cracking it where it landed.

Duke quickly recovered and with a slashing stroke caught Tanous on the arm. Blood spurted out, but Tanous's strong black armour saved his arm.

"What manner of sword is that?" asked Tanous as he quickly recovered and knocked the sword away with his other arms black platted armour.

The next action saw both Tanous and Duke's swords clash together, but on contact the Sorcerer's Sword glowed bright blue and the long sword held by Tanous broke in two at the point of contact. A part of it fell to the floor with a loud CLANG!

Tanous was not giving up however and inflicted a gash across Duke's stomach cutting through Dukes armour with the broken sword.

Duke pulled back to avoid any further damage to himself – the cut was not deep but it stung and bleed as if it were.

Before Tanous could inflict a more fatal wound Benedict responded with a smashing blow of his staff to Tanous's head.

"CLUNK!" as the staff made contact with the helmet sending Tanous to the floor unconscious.

"Enough Duke! We have work to do," replied Benedict. "Let me have a look at that wound," referring to Duke's bleeding stomach.

Benedict looked at it carefully before taking some strips of cloth from his own cloak and adding special oil from his shoulder sack to them. Wrapping it around the wound tightly he stopped any flow of blood and Duke felt a lot better.

"A wound like that will take a good few sunrises to heal properly," he said. You will have to be more careful when you are next playing!"

Duke smiled weakly, "I guess we have to continue upwards?"

"No one seems to have heard anything," said Pazamor.

"No, because the walls of such a tower as this are built so thick that they would muffle any such sounds," said Benedict.

"What of a way of escape?" asked Pazamor.

"I am working on it," replied Duke, always the planner, as they continued up the winding steps of Dagmar's Tower.

After they got half way up the tower a door opened and an alchemist appeared. "What do you want?" he snapped. "The tower is out of limits to soldiers – go back to your barracks."

"We have a message for Kraytos."

"Well he is in the top most point of the tower but if you should anger him by disturbing his work unnecessarily then you will find yourself at the bottom of the tower very quickly," laughed the alchemist.

The group continued up the steps until they found the top most door on a small landing.

They approached it carefully.

"This is just like the game chess," whispered Benedict, "capture the King and it is all over!"

"Exactly!" responded Duke as he tried to find a handle to open the door, but was unsuccessful.

"Pazamor?" asked Benedict as if to say 'can you deal with this problem?'

Pazamor looked carefully at the door, he thought for a while. No handles were evident - so he knocked hard on it, to Benedict and Duke's horror.

"Go away!" said the voice behind it, "unless you have finished with my toys."

"Well this is the problem, we have found a fault in the construction," replied Pazamor.

The door opened in the same way the doors of the front of the tower slid open, to reveal a tall man, dressed in a black cloak before them.

"There is no error in my construction they are perfect! What do you really want?" he asked suspiciously.

"Well that is the problem," said Pazamor, "we need something that will breakdown or need recharging. That way people will need to come back to you as King and Master."

Kraytos put his hand to his chin and moved his fingers across it so they came together as he pondered the proposal.

"That is actually an excellent suggestion – but half of my required toys have already gone to the main towns and villages in our land. It is too late to make such suggested modifications, unless... When I use the mind control unit I could make those under my control pick up the next model from me. Those that don't could be disposed of – excellent proposal! But WHO ARE YOU?"

"We are merchants that have come from affair travelling by passage of a pirate ship to trade and make a profit. You being a wizard – we thought that you might pay for such knowledge," responded Duke quickly.

"I might," replied Kraytos, still pondering if they might be spies or really whom they say.

'You are mercenary merchants?' he thought to himself, still pondering – they could be he thought, looking at the rough way they were dressed.

"Ok," he finally said, "but first you will need to speak to 'Tanous', my chief of security, and if you are who you say you are then you may stay but if you are not, then you will speak to my Constable instead," (suggesting the dungeon).

Pazamor stared at the large concave mirror in front of them and the throne like-chair. It was as if he intuitively knew what Kraytos was up to.

"Our brother here has something to show you. Can you pass me the artefact Brother?" asked Pazamor.

At first Brother Benedict was confused but then he understood and passed Pazamor the Kings seal from around his neck.

"Our Brother will 'assist you'," said Pazamor.

Brother Benedict smiled at Pazamor and while Kraytos was examining the seal and had just recognised what it was and also that this had indeed all been a ruse, Benedict brought his staff into contact with the back of Kraytos's head.

Kraytos crumpled to the floor unconscious.

"This will give us some more time," said Duke, but not much.

Pazamor looked at Kraytos's throne more carefully. "Give me a hand Duke he said. "Can you take out that big crystal from the top of the throne with your dagger, being careful not to damage it?"

"Ah, I will help you Duke," said Benedict, recognising that it would be glued in some way. Benedict poured some black liquid he took from his shoulder sack onto the stone and rubbed it in and around the edges, as together, he and Duke tried to force it from the throne.

"Can I have the Sorcerer's Sword?" asked Pazamor.

Duke passed the sword to Pazamor, who took hold of the handle and located the secret switch that had enabled him to lock the stone in place. The same switch realised the gemstone.

The large crystal that Duke was now preying with a knife popped out and Benedict grabbed it.

"Excellent!" said Pazamor, "now I need something sticky!"

He thought for a moment, after handing the sword back to Duke, then grabbing his sack, scrapped the bottom of it with his hand and brought out a white powdered substance.

"Flour?" asked Benedict.

"Exactly!" exclaimed Pazamor, as he spat onto his hand and rubbed this and the flour together creating a paste. He took the paste and gemstone and placed this into the hole that Duke had made behind the crystal with his knife. Pazamor carefully put the paste all around the hole to hold the crystal back in place over the top of this, as if nothing had been moved.

"I think I see your plan Pazamor," said Benedict – "now what of escape?"

"That's my department!" replied Duke.

The next minute the door was being pounded on, "Open up Master there are intruders in the castle grounds and the King is missing!" It was Tanous, whom had now partially recovered from his unannounced sleep.

"Quick! Rip the tapestries off!" said Duke to Benedict, "Pazamor follow me."

They each took one of the large ornate tapestries of battle scenes from the wall and followed Duke through a trap door to the top most part of the tower.

Below them they could hear and see lots of guards moving towards the tower.

"I hope this isn't the plan I think it is Duke?" said Benedict, looking down the steep drop before them.

All of a sudden a massive ball of fire landed in the grounds of the castle, exploding and sending out smaller balls of fire all around it. Panic set in around them as all realised the castle itself was under attack.

"Sapphira!" said Benedict.

"Just on time!" said Duke quickly tying two ends of the tapestry together, with some tassels that extended from the ends, and that helped him form a triangle from it.

"Now follow meeeee!" as he leapt from the tower holding the tapestry wooden edges in each hand and gliding like a giant seagull back towards the Keep.

Pazamor did the same and followed, as he leapt off the end he could see two large boats in the distance and what looked like a giant catapult that stretched across them both. Their masts must have been utilised in its construction and replaced by oars, such was their size. Sapphira had clearly assisted the King and many loyal soldiers from Port Kepland in helping build it in such short time.

Benedict hesitated but when he saw the trap door they had just come from open with armed guards approaching, he quickly changed his mind and followed.

As they glided towards the Keep another massive fireball flew over the castle wall and directly in front of them smashing into the Keep's door and some of its remains even rolling into the Keep.

All around panic set in. The tent the wraith had been using to control some of the people burnt down from some of the smaller fire balls that had come from the large ball, revealing the full light of the sun that quickly turned the wraith to dust.

Kraytos appeared at the top of the tower now and all could see he was really angry with what was going on.

"Kill them!" he shouted in maddened anger.

But not everyone was eager to listen to him. Many were unwilling conscripts and seeing a chance of escape took it, as another great ball knocked a hole in the main wooden door of the castle, just as the portcullis happened to be open. The last shipment of Kraytos's upmarket toys leaving through this. Those that didn't want to be there ran out of that gate faster than anyone else could respond to their escape. There was clearly too much confusion and commotion going on within the castle walls to deal with all of the problems at once.

As Duke, Pazamor and Benedict hit the ground Duke quickly threw away the burning tapestry he had landed with, it having caught on fire from a stray ball of fire from one of the bigger balls.

In front of them the door was still on fire, but a big enough hole remained to grant access.

"The main gate is open Duke!"

"Yes, but I prefer the back door!"

They all exited the way they had come and before the end of the day had managed to re-group at the Black Swan to rest and discuss further their plans.

Chapter 16
Dagmar's Tower

While in the corner of the room next to a comfy wooden fire, where Jack the Rabbit lay slumped on a table, Sapphira took out a small, clear spherical crystal from a battered sack and threw this within the fire nearby. Shadows once again danced within the small ball as Sapphira concentrated on an image of Torrum to send a message telepathically.

In the next moment all the group could see Torrum clearly within the crystal ball.

"What are all these tetrahedron toys turning up in Wizards' Way?" he asked, "People are buying them like the latest fashion craze!"

Pazamor answered, "Although they may seem like harmless toys they are mini, mental transmitters. I think that Kraytos is aiming to take over as many minds as he can through them and launch an attack on the Troll Kingdom."

"Kraytos has never forgiven the trolls for what has happened in the past Pazamor. It does not surprise me, but unless he finds forgiveness in his heart then the cycle of Karma shall not be broken and death shall follow death," sighed Torrum.

"Well if he tries to use this power to control others he will find it controlling him!" said Pazamor, "as the Sorcerer's stone is connected to the main transmission point, the throne he would intend to use as his seat of control."

"That is very clever Pazamor! It could well work but we must at least give him the chance of surrender before he attempts to destroy others and in so doing destroys himself," replied Torrum.

"So what is the game plan?" asked Duke, sword in hand.

Sapphira laughed, "We are fighting a wizard, not a warrior Duke."

"Not so hasty Sapphira, Duke's willingness to serve and fearlessness in battle are worthy contenders for one that might hide their weaknesses behind a cloak."

Sapphira blushed, "Yes of course Master."

"It seems to me your power lies in the group, and not in the individual. You all have different strengths but by working together you bring about the needed results. That good can prevail were real friendships exist – that thing you call love."

"Are you getting all soppy on us Torrum?" laughed Duke.

Sapphira turned her head as if to disagree with Duke.

"I think you are right," spoke Benedict finally. "It has been my experience that the power of group energy is far superior to that of the individual. While we brothers believe in ourselves we are also untied in our belief of the Universal Spirit and understand our connectedness to its love and peace. We will only kill to defend, and then only when a life is threatened."

"Ok Master I understand that you wish us to try and gain the surrender of Kraytos, but how do you intend us to do this?" asked Sapphira.

Torrum sighed deeply, "My child you must find the answer yourselves I can only give you the direction – you must travel the path..." the picture faded and the group found themselves starring at a blank crystal ball again.

"One of us could go back to the castle carrying a white flag and asking Kraytos to surrender nicely," said Duke with a smile.

"That is not one of your better plans Duke," replied Sapphira.

"How about we capture some Kraytos Demons and get them to dig us a tunnel inside the castle walls!" said Pazamor.

"While capturing the demons may prove difficult getting them to do what you want even more so as they are under the command of Kraytos," said Sapphira.

Pazamor thought, "Not exactly! They are under the control of Kraytos's miner bird, which is under the control of Kraytos – if we control the bird then we control the demons."

"Pazamor is right," said Benedict finally, "control of the miner bird will give us control of the demons."

"But how do we capture such a bird?"

Sapphira thought for a while, "We get Torrum to send a message via his miner bird. Kraytos will not suspect anything and give a message via return and we will have the opportunity to enchant the bird for our own use."

"That sounds like Karmic retribution for Lord Kraytos," smiled Benedict.

"Indeed," said Duke.

"Can you send the message to Torrum on what we need Sapphira?" asked Benedict.

Sapphira closed her eyes for a minute, "It is done," she said.

"Well we will have to wait for nightfall before we can capture the demons," let us get some sleep here tonight.

Sapphira approached the Tavern Keeper and paid enough money for two rooms, one for her and Benedict and the other for Duke and Pazamor.

"Good night gentleman," she said, "we will need to awaken very early in the morning before sunrise if we are to capture some dangerous demons," nodding her head as she left for the room.

Benedict once again settled down to pray and meditate, while Duke ordered a pint of ale for himself and Pazamor, having bartered a small silver dagger from the castle armoury.

"Thanks," said Pazamor.

"You are welcome Paz," said Duke holding up his tankard to Pazamor's health and clanking it.

Duke walked over to see Jack the Rabbit, while Pazamor took out his battered book and began to read:

Enjoy life...
Look at the beauty of nature around you and find peace and tranquillity within it and within you.

Be detached in life so that the things of life do not attach to you. 'By giving up things you receive'.

If you try to possess energy it will destroy you. Avoid obsession and be detached, intelligently using it for the good of others.

'Seek not to control least you be controlled'.

Without energy nothing can happen – use it creatively for best effect but do not waste it by calling upon it blindly and not using it or it can destroy you.

People try to amass wealth, often in the form of money, money itself having energy behind it. But this is bad – all energy should be shared in some way. Think of it like a football and you will see an idea of how it works if you intend to succeed in scoring a goal you will need to pass the ball to others before it can come back to you. Failure to do this will often mean someone or something will end up taking it away from you.

'Life is sometimes like a bar of soap – if you hold on to it too tight it will jump out of your hands!'

Pazamor closed the book and found his room to retire to. Although very small it was suited to what he was used to and sat down to meditate on what he had read and the day's events, before going asleep.

It must have been past the dead of night and sometime early in the morning when Sapphira ran into Pazamor and Duke's room shaking them both to awaken.

"Come on!" she said, "time to get up friends." Sapphira had a small black bird on her shoulder and Benedict was waiting in the doorway.

"Yawnnn!" said Duke as he staggered up and grabbed his things.

"You did it then!" said Pazamor motioning towards the miner bird.

"Not exactly, Torrum partially enchanted the bird, enough to make it think it needed to give me a message from Kraytos, but yes, now the bird is under our control for a time."

*

The group found themselves inside the graveyard and on a tombstone for protection. Within a short space of time four Kraytos Demons appeared and Sapphira quickly enchanted them through the voice of the miner bird. She gave them instructions to cut a tunnel large enough for them to walk through, spanning the distance to the castle walls of Castle Dronagon.

The four demons cut holes above each other as if they were on top of each other and although it was a tight fit as tunnels go, it was indeed possible to walk through but the group needed to be mindful of acid remains. They covered themselves with cloth and their cloaks for protection as they travelled, Sapphira leading, after creating a light spell in front of them to guide their way.

"Your plan is working Pazamor – well done,"

"I still think the white flag idea would have been a good one," joked Duke.

[They all laughed].

After what must have only been half a morning's travel, they found themselves inside some sort of inner walls.

The Kraytos demons having dug through were stood erect, ears over their faces, waiting for the next command.

"Where are we?" asked Duke.

"This is a little small to be the castle walls and look at the shape – it is triangular!"

"Off course!" said Benedict. "We are inside the giant tetrahedron that was being built within the castle walls – Kraytos must have finished it."

Sapphira instructed the Demons to dig again and they soon found themselves outside the walls of the tetrahedron and inside the walls of the large castle complex.

"Well this is a turn up for the books!" said a voice from behind them.

It was Kraytos and he had Tanous and an army of about twenty soldiers with him.

"I was just about to test my new toy and you lot turn up again like a bad day," said Kraytos. "Well it is your last day – get them Tanous!"

Tanous roared the command for his guards to attack.

Sapphira counter commanded the four Kraytos Demons to attack the guards and protect them through the miner bird. This subsequently ignored her and instead flew over to Lord Kraytos.

"Mine I think!" he said, as the bird flew over to him and perched on his shoulder. [Having telepathically commanded it such].

Tanous and the black guard continued to advance. Benedict quickly produced his staff, extending it to its full length with two strong flicks of his hand. Duke took his small crossbow in one hand and the Sorcerer's Sword in the other, holding this high it invoked the power of the moon, as if surrounded by such an aura – the Kraytos Demons froze – just starring at the sword. Even without the gem the sword had power.

Sapphira quickly conjured Haddon and started to mix potions at the ready from her belt.

Pazamor had no weapons to hand, but a short sword given to him by Duke and stopped for a moment, praying to the Universal Spirit that this fight might end with no bloodshed.   Then he simply stood in front of the two groups held out the palms of his hands vertically, with arms extended to both groups in a gesture of power and shouted in a commanding voice – "STOPPP!"

It was as if time stood still when he did this and that it was not his authority of which he spoke but rather that of the

Universal Spirit speaking through him, of which he had just invoked by speaking from his heart.

"Enough!"

Both groups stood down to listen to what Pazamor had to say to them.

"Would you kill your own brother and sister? Do you fight for yourself or for another? If you look within your hearts is it not YOU that is the centre of the world in which you live and have your Being?   If this is so why do you follow the commands of another whom does not believe in you but only in himself. A man that would simply use you for his own means and then discard you when no longer needed - like a piece of rubbish.

We stand here today together as citizens of Dronagon's Domain not Kraytos's and it is King Dronagon whom we still follow - is it not?" Holding up the chain with the seal of King Dronagon for all to see.

"Which of you would fight against himself?"

More than half of the guards were now in doubt and confused as to why they would attack someone or a group that held the seal of the King.

"He lies!" shouted Kraytos at the top of his voice. "They have killed the King and that is why he has the King's seal. They have come to steal this castle from us. Kill the traitors!"

Sapphira did not wait for another word from Kraytos in the time that Pazamor and Kraytos had been speaking she had been casting a spell.

Pointing a finger at Kraytos she shouted, "Actomos – Vantamos!" and blew with her mouth. She did the same in the direction of the guards and as she did so Haddon ran around Kraytos and the group of guards in the figure of an 8.

He flew so fast that he disappeared from sight, or at least from the sight of the few that could see him, namely Sapphira, Pazamor and Kraytos.

Instead of Haddon there was now a large wind that flew around Kraytos and the guards. It picked up dust and dirt from the floor and surrounded them blinding them all and making it impossible to see anything in front or behind them. Some of the guards dropped to the floor to avoid being blown away, the wind was so strong, like a tornado and attempted to lift the guards in the air, despite their heavy armour.

In the battlements several guards had let off a hail of arrows and crossbow bolts, which flew towards the group. Benedict ran around them with lightning speed, protecting them by deflecting as many of the arrows as he could with his staff. Sapphira used her cloak in the same way as her first encounter with the enchanted black guard, by holding up her cloak, several arrows hit it and stopped dead, falling to the ground as if they had hit an impenetrable wall. She extended her cloak to cover others in the group, as the arrows intensified.

Duke fired the odd well aimed bolt at several guards in the battlements, knocking them from their position with direct hits.

"Retreat!" shouted Duke, just as Kraytos's Odil had appeared and stopped the tornado surrounding him - though too late for the miner bird, which lay dead beside him. The Kraytos demons being released from their spell disappeared down the hole from which they had come; no one having control over them anymore.

The group quickly retreated following the demons down the large hole but turned within the tunnel created to get back inside the pyramidal structure, from where they had been earlier.

"Seal the hole!" shouted Kraytos as Odil had just freed the guards from the tornado surrounding them by knocking Haddon out of the way; Haddon disappearing in a puff of light.

The guards took some large stones that had been left from the construction of the large tetrahedron and threw them into the hole until it was quite full.

"Excellent! said Kraytos, "Now - to rule the world!" he spoke, as he made his way to Dagmar's Tower, madly laughing to himself.

*

Within the dark sealed walls Sapphira conjured a light spell. Their eyes accustomed to the new light within the walls of the building.

Duke knocked at some of the stone wall with the handle of a dagger. "Quite solid!" he said.

Benedict also looked closely but more to the top of the structure. "Silver!" he announced, pointing at the large silver cable that extended from the roof to the epicentre of the room, of which looked like a large roughly cut ball of crystal was extended, with two giant black slabs of stone parallel to this, held by wooden supports, cradling the crystal within.

A further silver cable came out of the crystals centre and extended to a corner of the building to a large silver disk, the size of a large shield, held by a wooden post which extended from the floor and then the cable through the centre of this disk and through the floor. Opposite this large disk was another of the same size but its composition was gold and it faced the face of one of the tetrahedrons triangular sides.

"It looks familiar," replied Duke, pointing at the silver disk.

They all thought for a moment then Benedict spoke, "It's the same type of mirror we saw at Troll Tower and it is also very similar to the one we have in the Celthina Monastery, in the highest tower. Pazamor do you still have your map?"

Pazamor took a crumpled piece of paper from his sack of which they all looked at intently.

"Look!" said Pazamor – "A triangle!"

"So it is!" said Benedict. The others slowly realising what Pazamor and Benedict could see.

"If you look at the position of the Celthina Monastery, Troll Tower and Dagmar's Tower they form a triangle. This triangular building must be a transmitter of some kind and they must some how link up to it energetically – how though?" pondered Pazamor aloud.

"Let's break the link then!" suggested Duke holding up the Sorcerer's Sword.

"A simple cut to these cables should do it," responded Benedict.

Sapphira finally responded, "Kraytos is trying to utilise the mental plane. The shape of the tetrahedron can channel such energies in the same way a pyramid can channel astral energies he is trying to link human minds up through his toys, channel them through the other silver disks in the towers to this point of the tetrahedron, the gold disk is the point of exit facing Dagmar's tower and his seat of power. He is looking to enchant the majority of Dronagon's Domain through these devices – it could very well work. I must inform my Master!"

Sapphira went to one of the uncluttered corners of the room sat in a meditative posture and created a link with herself and her Master through fire and her crystal ball.

Duke was about to slash at the silver cables when they all became aware of another entity in the room.

"Odil!" said Sapphira, as a dim ball of light could be seen flying through the wall towards Duke.

Duke grabbed his sword and swung it towards the source of light as he did so Sapphira began to cast a spell on Duke to enable him to see Odil. Suddenly Duke could see everything in a golden light and Odil was clearly stood before him with some sort of crystal staff, which he used to deflect Dukes blow of the sword.

Odil swung the staff around in a counter attack but on second contact with the sword it shattered into pieces. Only Duke could fully see Odil, but the rest of the group could see flashes of coloured lights from the clashes of the sword and staff in the other dimension.

"Look!" said Pazamor pointing at the silver cable in the ground, it was glowing with a blue aura and giving off a dull buzz.

"Kraytos has started," announced Benedict.

Odil continued to fight Duke, if now only with two bits of staff, one in each hand. He used it in a cross position to stop one attacking blow which came down towards his head and pushed away the Sorcerer's Sword with both hands.

The next move was a thrust attack from Odil, using one part of the staff as a shield and the other as a spear he deflected one blow from Duke and counter thrust with his right arm. The broken staff ripped through Dukes black armour and embedded itself in his ribs.

By now the crystal in the centre of the room was beginning to glow and the humming noise could be heard to intensify from the energy building up, brought to it from the silver cable in the ground.

Odil now turned his attention to Pazamor, as Duke lay on the floor incapacitated from the last deadly blow.

Pazamor felt a huge cramp in his stomach as Odil thrust the remaining piece of his staff into him with all his astral force.

Sapphira laid her physical body still on the floor and suddenly she appeared in the astral world in which Odil was working.

Odil continued the assault on Pazamor but kept an eye on Sapphira, least she joined in the attack. However, Sapphira had already made her attack more stealthily by sending Haddon on ahead to Dagmar's Tower.

Haddon having found Odil's room and physical body, had been sent to wake him, however, by accident, Haddon knocked a candle to the floor, which managed to light a tapestry on the wall. Soon all the contents of the room were on fire and even the bed on which Odil lay was alight.

The first sign Odil actually knew of this was when he felt very warm, but had no time to react to this having to concentrate so hard to remain in the astral. His energy level felt depleted. A swinging blow he made at Pazamor only seemed to go through him instead of making contact.

He looked at Sapphira again – what had she done to him – he was much less effective now.

Sapphira simply stood looking at him and sighed.

He struck at her but had little effect as his hand went right through her astral body also, causing no damage at all.

"What is going on?" he asked her.

"Because of your love of this false astral world you are now banished to it for a greater length of time – at least until you can be re-born. You have clearly lost contact with your own physical body – you are dead!"

"What do you..." Odil disappeared from view flying back to where the remains of his body lay...

"NOOO!" he screamed knocking over some objects from the physical world in his anger and then disappearing into blackness and a deep sleep...

Benedict stood over Pazamor, "Are you alright friend?"

Pazamor felt his stomach, "Other than stomach cramp I am fine, thanks Ben."

They went over to Duke who lay on the floor; he was holding his stomach too.

Sapphira was also back in the physical by now.

"How is he?" she asked Benedict, as he took off Duke's armour and oil soaked cloth to reveal a badly bruised stomach in the area he had been hit with the crystal staff in the astral world.

"If it had been the real world Duke would be dead now and even in the astral if he had been a weaker person we would be looking at an empty shell.

Duke sat up, groaning, "Well you won't get rid of me that easily," he said coughing and laughing, with difficulty.

"Where is the one that attacked me?"

"He is nothing more than a ghost now duke, having lost his body – he is earth bound and will be stuck to that tower for a long time," replied Sapphira.

"Help me up let us find a way out of this prison."

"Keep away from the path of the crystal and the gold disc," warned Sapphira.

"Yes," said Pazamor, "it is probably the exit point like the silver is 'in' the gold is 'out'..."

By now the crystal was glowing brighter and the humming noise much, much louder.

Duke looked for the Sorcerer's Sword and finding it beside him, picked it up.

"No Duke!" said Sapphira. Duke being about to cut the silver cable.

A blinding flash of white light left the crystal and shot towards the gold disc and then from this it blasted forth through the pyramidal structure and towards Dagmar's Tower.

"ARRRRRRRAH!" could be heard screaming from that direction and then the light stopped and the room went dark again.

*

Much time later the group could hear movement at the top of the structure and light burst into the darkness as several of the top stones were knocked out of the way. Ropes were extended down and the group climbed out, helped by soldiers, to meet Torrum and King Dronagon.

"I thank you for restoring my kingdom to me and avoiding yet another war with the trolls," said King Dronagon.

"Kraytos is no more," replied Torrum, "He has lost his mind and is no longer a threat to us or this Domain - only to himself."

"He will now be my guest," said the King motioning some guards to take him away to the dungeons.

Kraytos left mumbling something about - "Too much light, too much light." His hair stood on end like a cat that raises its hair in self-defence.

Torrum handed Pazamor the Sorcerer's Stone, "yours I think!" he said, as he handed it to Pazamor, "Keep it safe you may need it again someday."

It still glowed blue.

"Thanks!" said Pazamor.

"Where is Tanous?" asked Duke.

"He and a few untrusted guards ran off before we stormed the castle – they took a pirate ship and left our kingdom. Just as well because they are no longer welcome here and should they return they will also be guests in my dungeon," replied the King.

"Your majesty your kingdom has been saved by the courage and bravery of a dedicated few – can you reward them in some way?" reported Torrum.

"Why of course Torrum, let each stand forth and ask what they want and I will try to grant their wish as best I can, as they have granted mine."

Sapphira was first: "I wouldn't mind a tower of my own," she said.

Benedict stood forth: "I would like access to the King's secret library to be able to borrow some books on behalf of my Master."

Duke had his hand to his mouth in a pondering mode: "A castle of my own would be good," he said with a big smile on his face.

"And you Pazamor? What would you like from me?" asked the King.

"I would like you to give my mother her house so that she doesn't need to pay tax on it or our land anymore."

The King stopped for a moment, as if to consider each of the requests, and then gave his decisions:

"You Sapphira, want a Wizard's Tower? Well until you can build your own you may have Dagmar's Tower. It is empty now and I would rather have a wizard I can trust living in it than none at all.

You Brother Benedict may have the key to my secret library and go as you please but may only borrow two books at a time and can only have more after you return the ones you have copied or read.

You Duke, I would like to be my personal guard. You can live in this castle as if it where your own but it is still the property of our Domain and under my rule.

You Young Pazamor..." – the space shimmered around the King.

"You Young Pazamor asked for something to help another instead of yourself. You could have asked for materialistic things like gold or silver but opted to ask for something of more value something that will bring real happiness to another. By releasing them of a chain they have. In so doing you will find that you too have increased freedom to roam these lands and find within them your real Self."

The space shimmered around the King again: "Thank you all for your help." Apart from granting them all their requests, in some form or another, he gave each a bag of gold. He also gave two guards each with horses to Benedict and Pazamor, to return them safely home.

"But first let us celebrate with a feast in the Great Hall shouted the King." All around clapped and cheered as the group soon found themselves together again, dinning at the King's table, that was laid with so many different types of food.

The King paid tribute to the House Steward for the feast lay before them and they started after a brief prayer.

Benedict thanked the Universal Spirit for the food supplied and long-term friendships formed in working together for the greater good of all.

Several musicians performed before them as they ate better than they had done so since starting out on their journey.

Duke sipped some wine while eating a piece of chicken while Benedict had some fish. Sapphira was content with some sort of nut and mushroom dish, as was Pazamor.

"I hope I will not miss that friendship you talked of earlier Ben," said Pazamor.

Sapphira laughed, "We can still see each other at night – remember?"

That was just the point Pazamor did not remember his dreams so well – but he understood what Sapphira meant.

Pazamor wondered if their friendship would be broken through the distance of time or whether they would all stay together as friends until the day they died.

A servant brought some more drinks to the table, as he came to Pazamor the space around him shimmered.

"The Universal Spirit is all around you. Find me in all things and you will never lack real friends. Though some may seem to leave others may appear and if you see me in them then you will never lose friends. Their faces may change in the passage of time but that which is in their heart is the same which is in yours – love transcends all."

The shimmer left the servant and he attended to others at the table. Pazamor laughed out loud. Torrum smiled, "Do you understand life better now? He asked Pazamor.

"Are you Tang?" asked Pazamor of Torrum.

Torrum asked the same question of Sapphira.

"Indeed he is Pazamor – in as much as in that the same Universal Spirit that is in Torrum is also in us all."

Pazamor felt that Torrum was playing games having not specifically given him an answer.

"So what is the payment today? - for answering your question," asked Torrum of Pazamor.

Pazamor smiled.

Chapter 17
Home Coming

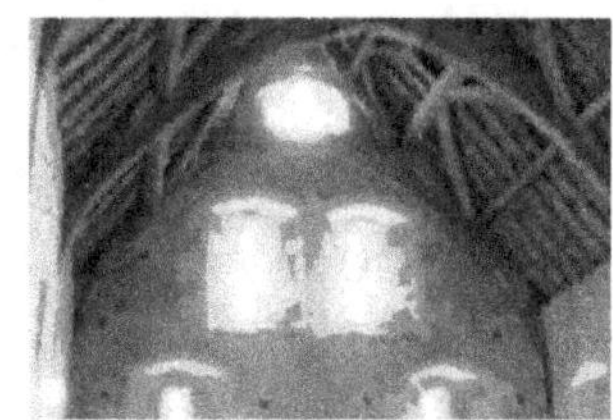

About four sunrises latter Pazamor was at home with his mother having told her of his adventures and the good news of the king's pardon - of the free house and land rent, which had been put under the control of Squire Duke – Pazamor's close friend.

His mother found it hard to believe at first but when the guards that accompanied him agreed to this being the truth and Pazamor shared some of the gold he had with his mother she had to agree. She hugged her son and thanked the Universal Spirit for his safe return. She also handed the guards a couple of gold coins each for accompanying Pazamor on the journey home.

"Are ye go'n ta be leav'n me then Pazamor?" she finally asked after the guards had gone.

"I will be gone for a while again at some point but I like your food too much to totally leave you mother." They both laughed.

"Well see if ye can find a good woman and settle down me love. Don't spend half ye life in ideal dreaming."

"I will do my best mother – you can trust me to do that."

"Ye are a good son love. Thank ye for all ye help."

They both hugged each other again before Pazamor returned to bed tired from the long journey home.

As Pazamor lay on his soft bed of hay and began to drift off to sleep.   He found himself waking up within his dream again.   He was sat at a familiar marble table with thirteen stone seats surrounding it.

Torrum was sat at the head seat, with Sapphira to his left, Benedict, Duke and Katrina.   But who were the other seven seats for?

"Are we all ready for the next task in hand?" asked Torrum.

The group responded by looking at each other and chanting, ***"For the love of good and for the good of love do we work."***

Pazamor slept deeply...

ADDENDUM

It is hoped that when you read this book you will find within it another book, one in which you may discover and compare your own life's experiences to that within. That, like Pazamor, through your own 'mind's eye', you may come to 'realise' answers to your own deep searching questions. That this book may break the chains of conditioning all around you and open your mind, heart and soul to the beauty of not only the magical, physical world of nature but also the very real spiritual world behind and in front of this.

Chakras

Crown Chakra
Ajna Chakra

Throat Chakra

Heart Chakra

Solar Plexus

Sacral Centre

Base Chakra

Recommended Reading

Creme, B. (1990) ***Maitreya's Mission.*** London: Share International Foundation. (ISBN 90-71484-06-8)

Creme, B. (1998) ***Transmission: A Meditation For The New Age.*** London: Share International Foundation. (ISBN 90-71484-17-3)

Steiner. R. (1984) ***Occult Science an outline.*** Kent: Whitstable Litho Ltd. (ISBN 0-85440-440-6)

Besant, A, and Leadbeater, C. (1986) **Thought Forms.** Adyar: The Theosophical Publishing House. (ISBN 0-8356-0008-4)

Leadbeater, C. (1987) **The Astral Plane.** Adyar: The Theosophical Publishing House. (ISBN 81-7059-067-1)

Canfield, J. and Hansen, M. (1993) **Chicken Soup for the Soul.** Florida: Health Communications Inc. (ISBN 1-55874-262-X)